THE ART OF BEING FRIENDS

(A PACT BETWEEN THE FORGOTTEN, #1)

JESSICA SORENSEN

 Created with Vellum

PROLOGUE

RAVEN

I'VE ALWAYS SUFFERED from insomnia, even before my parents died. Tonight is no exception.

After spending hours trying to go to sleep, I end up lying in bed for quite a while, just staring up at the ceiling and thinking. I have no plans of moving anytime soon until I hear the strangest noise coming from outside. It almost sounds like a fire crackling.

Confused, I get up, tiptoe over to the window, and peer outside, surprised to find that, yep, the noise is indeed exactly what I thought it was.

A fire is crackling in the middle of the field beside my house. A man stands beside it. A man who looks an awful lot like my uncle, who has been my guardian ever since my parents died.

I watch from the window as he throws something into the flames, then steps back.

What the hell?

What is he burning in the middle of the night? Whatever it is, it can't be good. Why else would anyone burn something in the middle of the night?

My best bet is that it might be some incriminating evidence against him. My uncle may be a police officer, but he does a lot of sketchy stuff.

I stand by the window for a bit, watching as he remains in front of the flames. Eventually, he puts the fire out by shoveling dirt onto it. Then he starts back toward the house.

I hunker down to avoid being seen. Then, when I hear the front door creak open, I crawl back toward my bed and climb in. And it's a good thing I do, too.

Moments later, my bedroom door is opened.

I keep my eyes shut, but I can sense someone looking at me. It has to be my uncle, but what the hell is he doing?

My side aches as worry creeps through me. What if he's contemplating cutting me again? He already did it once this week, carved the word *freak* into my side with a knife, his form of punishment whenever I do something bad, which seems to be all the time.

Eventually, he leaves my room, and I let out a shaky breath and try to force myself to go to sleep. It proves to be impossible, though, so I eventually sneak out to see if I can figure out what he was burning.

After slipping on a jacket and shoes, I climb out the window and shimmy down the tree beside it. Then I tiptoe over to the spot where the fire was. I use the flashlight on my phone to look around the area, but all I can find are embers. Whatever he was burning, disintegrated in the flames. Or, well, maybe not.

Something shiny and silver catches my eye.

I crouch down, scoop it up, and then my confusion doubles. It's a pendant shaped like a feather.

Weird.

I'm not sure if this is what he was trying to burn, but it's pretty, so I decide to keep it. Then I head back into the house, telling myself that, come morning, I'll sneak out and see if I can find anything else he may have been burning.

Of course, when the sun rises, and I get up and go downstairs, my uncle announces we're moving out of town. And not in a few weeks, but in a few days, which is odd since him and my aunt always talk about how much they love the town we live in now.

Even weirder is, when I sneak outside to check around where my uncle lit the fire last night, all signs of it are gone. Almost like I dreamt the incident. And I may have believed I had except, when I check the pocket of my pajamas, the pendant is still in there.

1

ONE WEEK LATER

RAVEN

A LOT of people say my name has a magical sound to it. I guess it does.

I used to love my name. Ravenlee Wilowwynter; Raven for short. It's different. Unique. Pretty even. But it also has a deeper meaning. Or, well, an actual raven does.

Bad luck.

That's what those birds represent. And right after I turned twelve, I realized this. Because, like those dark-feathered birds, I became bad luck. Cursed even. Because I'm the reason my parents died. I'm the reason they're buried beneath the ground. I'm the reason they aren't here anymore.

These guilty thoughts creep through my mind as I stand in front of the mirror, examining my long, dark hair that looks similar to the dark shade of a raven's feather—

midnight black, with hints of violet and blue when it catches the light. I can't help questioning if I used to be a raven in another life. Perhaps that's why I bring bad luck wherever I go.

"Ravenlee Wilowwynter! Get your butt down here," my aunt Beth shouts from downstairs. "You don't need to make everyone else late for the first day of school because you can't get your lazy butt moving."

My initial instinct is to throw back a snarky retort, but I know better than to do that while my uncle's home. So, I take a deep breath before calling out, "I'm just about ready."

She doesn't say anything to me directly, but I hear her tell my uncle, "That damn girl is really getting on my nerves. She's always late. And don't even get me started on how much trouble she gets into. And the mouth on her … I don't understand why we can't kick her butt out when she turns eighteen. I don't think I can put up with her crap until graduation."

"I agreed when I took her in, Beth. She's going to live with us until she graduates from high school, and that's final," my uncle Don replies in a cold tone.

He's my dad's brother but, where my dad was a nice, caring man, my uncle is frigid and angry all the time, especially with me. Although there are occasions when he seems almost thrilled to be around me, but that's never a good thing.

"Now, go make me my breakfast. It's my first day, and I'm not going to be late."

I roll my eyes as my aunt says, "Of course, dear."

My aunt usually does what she's told, at least when it comes to my uncle. She stays home, where she cooks, cleans, and has dinner on the table every night when he gets home from work. I swear it's like they still think it's the 1950s or something. If I didn't despise my aunt so much, I might try to encourage her not to be such a doormat. But if I tried to tell her that, not only would my aunt ground my ass, my uncle would smack me a good one.

He's been doing that kind of shit since I moved in with them. At first, I put up a fight, trying to battle back, but a shit-ton of good that did. I quickly learned that fighting back meant more hits. So, I learned to swallow my pride and keep my mouth shut when I'm around my uncle. All bets are off, though, with everyone else.

I wish I had another choice. Wish I could turn him in. I thought about doing so when he first started smacking me around. The problem is that he's a cop. And I'm the rebel, piece of shit niece that they so kindly took in after she did horrible things. At least, that's how everyone sees it.

And I have a feeling things with my uncle are about to get even worse now that he's officially the sheriff of Honeyton, the small town that we moved to.

The place is out in the middle of nowhere,

surrounded by hills that give a sense of seclusion and friendliness. Well, that's the bullshit my uncle told us when he announced we were moving. Personally, I'm not buying it. I took a walk around town yesterday, and the looks I got from the townspeople were less than friendly. I could practically smell the judgment and snobbery lacing the crisp fall air and feel my impending outcast title waiting for me today when I enter the hallways of my new school. I do look kind of intimidating, though.

But it's cool. I can handle it. I can and have dealt with a lot worse. In fact, I'm used to being the outcast. I've been one since I moved in with my uncle, aunt, and their daughter, Dixie May.

Dixie fucking May. Though she's my cousin and is the same age as me, we have no other similarities. If I'm a reincarnated raven, then Dixie May is probably a hawk, which I once read are supposed to be predators to ravens and can represent danger. Honestly, from what I've read, ravens can usually only fend off a hawk if there's a group of them, also known as a conspiracy. I like the name conspiracy better, probably because I mentally conspire all the time to take Dixie May down. But I've never had any real friends, at least not long-lasting ones so, more than likely, that's not going to happen. Not that I just let her walk all over me. I don't at all.

Still, Dixie May is the most manipulative, fake, and devious person I've ever crossed paths with. She's also very pretty and charming when she needs to be, except at home where she acts like a spoiled brat. She also has ammunition against me—knows the reason I came to live with her and her family all those years ago. And when she told everyone at our old school about it, I instantly became labeled the freak that people not only despised but feared.

"Oh my God, I'm so sick of these damn boxes," Dixie May complains from her bedroom across the hall from mine. "I can't find anything. And my favorite pair of shoes are missing. I bet the movers stole them."

I roll my eyes. The movers were two big dudes who seemed nice enough, and in no way, shape, or form seemed like the kind of people who'd steal designer shoes. Not to mention, one single pair of shoes.

"I'll call and make a complaint," my aunt calls out to her.

"What's a freakin' complaint going to do?" Dixie May whines. "It won't get me my shoes back. And they were my favorite pair."

"I'm so sorry, sweetie," my aunt tells her. "If you want, we can drive over to the city this weekend and go shopping."

"Fine. But you better buy me a couple of extra pairs in case this happens again," Dixie May warns.

"Of course," my aunt says. "I'll even buy you a few new outfits if you want."

I'd roll my eyes again, but at this point, I'm starting to

worry that they'll get stuck in my head. For reals, though. Dixie May has so many clothes that my aunt and uncle had to add an extra closet to her room before we could move into this house.

Then there's me. My entire wardrobe fits into a bag and mostly consists of secondhand items that I purchased with money I saved up from jobs I worked here and there. But I like my clothes. They fit my personality, and when I wear them, I like to imagine who they used to belong to and what kind of life they had while they wore them.

Right now, I'm rocking a Nirvana shirt that I'm convinced someone wore to one of the band's concerts decades ago. I also have on a pair of cut-off shorts, knee-high tights, and clunky, scuffed boots that lace up all the way over my knees. I topped off the look with a plaid over-shirt and a leather jacket that used to belong to my mother. It's one of the few items I have left of hers. I like to occasionally breathe in the scent, pretending I can still smell her perfume.

I miss her so, so much.

As tears begin to well in my eyes, I suck them back and focus on finishing getting ready, putting on a velvet choker then adding leather bands to my wrists. I always wear them to cover up the scars marking my flesh.

Like always, my dark hair is swept to the side in a wild mess of waves, and I keep my makeup minimal, consisting of kohl eyeliner and some lip gloss—I'm not really a makeup sort of girl.

"Raven! You have one more minute to get your butt down here, and then we're leaving you!" Aunt Beth shouts, a warning ringing in her tone. "It's not like it's going to matter anyway. I'm sure I'll probably get a call from the school halfway through the day, informing me that, once again, you got yourself suspended."

She might be right. I do have a reputation for getting suspended. Most of the time, it's because I get into a fight, either from someone else starting it or I take the first swing after someone repeatedly called me names. I've had to go to anger management classes a couple times that, honestly, I'm not sure they helped.

It's not like I'm angry all the time. Most of the time, I can pull off indifference pretty damn well. But there's a particular name that really gets under my skin and, annoyingly, it's one of the words scarring my flesh beneath my clothes.

As my chest pressurizes at the memories of how the scars got there, I tear my gaze off the mirror, collect my bag, and then stick my hand underneath the mattress to grab a joint from my stash.

I have quite the collection under there. Most of it comes from my uncle. Remember how I said he does a lot of sketchy stuff? Well, bringing drugs home after he's done a bust is one of those things. He's been doing it for years, stealing a bit here and there then reporting that a less amount was found during a raid. How do I know this? Because I overheard a phone conversation once between him and one of his buddies. He didn't know I was home. I wasn't supposed to be, but I'd decided to ditch after a group of guys and girls jumped me and kicked my ass. I fought back, of course—my dad taught me how to protect myself at a young age—and I even got in a few good swings, but I was completely outnumbered. In the end, I gave someone a black eye and someone else a fat lip, while my face looked like a freakin' lumpy blueberry.

Anyway, I left school, went home, and hid up in my bedroom. My uncle had come home for lunch and, as I was sneaking around, trying to stay hidden, I noticed him empty some bags out of his pockets, stuffing them into the attic crawlspace. Then he called someone and informed them of what he had managed to bring home that day.

"I got a lot today," he said then paused. "Yeah, I know. I want you to push it as fast as you can."

Before my parents died, I'd been raised in a question-able neighborhood and knew enough about the drug world to understand what that meant.

When he left, I snuck up to the crawlspace and *jackpot*. I didn't take it all, just enough that he wouldn't notice. After that, it became a routine. Usually, I'd find only weed in there, but on a couple of occasions, I found some ecstasy or coke.

I'm a little worried about how things are going to work now that we've moved and he has a new job. I guess I'll find out. It's going to suck if he stops stealing drugs and stashing them in the house. Not that I'm addicted, but getting high often calms me, and I need help with that whenever I can.

"Raven! For the love of God, get down here!" Aunt Beth shouts furiously.

Sighing, I put the joint in my bag then head down the stairs to start what I'm sure is going to be a hellish first day of school.

2

RAVEN

I END up crossing paths with my uncle on my way out. He's in the kitchen, sitting at the table, eating breakfast and reading a newspaper. He doesn't look a lot like my dad—shorter and stockier with a bald spot on his head—which I'm grateful for. He's also dressed in his uniform.

I try to pass by the kitchen without being noticed and hurry toward the front door, but he glances up before I can make a quick exit.

His gaze sweeps across me, and then he frowns. "You're really going to go to school dressed like that?"

I bite back a rude remark and shrug while tugging on the sleeve of my jacket, mostly to keep the pendant hidden. It's the one I found in the remains of the fire, and I know it might be risky wearing it, but for some reason, I feel connected to it. Or maybe it's just that it's something nice, and it's been a while since I've had something nice.

He eyes me over again, making my skin crawl. "You look like a slut."

My anger ticks, and I want nothing more than to walk up and clock him in the face. But I fight the urge and turn for the door, preparing to walk out.

"You better not get into trouble today," he calls after me. "If you do, you'll be punished. I mean it, Ravenlee. You'll learn to obey, even if I have to—"

I rush out the front door and close it behind me, cutting off whatever threat he was about to throw my way. I might pay for the move later, but right now, all I want to worry about is getting through school, so I keep my head low and climb into the back seat of my aunt's car.

"God, it took you long enough. You can move so slow sometimes, Ravenlee," my aunt gripes as she drives down the driveway, heading for the main road.

I shrug and stare out the window, too tired to get into it with her right now.

I really need some coffee. And breakfast. Why did my uncle have to be in the kitchen this morning?

I zone out for most of the ride to school while Dixie May babbles about some reality TV show she's been watching. Aunt Beth occasionally joins in on the conversation, but Dixie May is usually the one to fill up the silence. The girl could probably break the world record with her ability to talk and talk and talk, especially about reality TV.

As soon as my aunt pulls up to the school, Dixie May's focus switches.

"This is seriously the school we have to go to?" She crinkles her nose at the brick building. "It's so small. And where the hell is student parking?"

"I'm sure it's around here somewhere," Aunt Beth tells her as she stops in the student drop-off area at the front. "Maybe at the back of the school."

Dixie May glares at her mother. "Well, they better have it, because there's no way in hell I'm parking Cutie in this tiny parking lot when it arrives."

Cutie is Dixie May's BMW that she got for her sixteenth birthday. Her parents didn't want her racking up miles on it when we moved, so they had it shipped over. It hasn't arrived yet, something Dixie complains about every day.

Me? I'm kind of grateful it hasn't arrived because, when it does, I have to go back to riding to school with her. And she usually ends up leaving me stranded after school, so I either have to walk home or catch the city bus. I don't think Honeyton has a city bus, which means I'll end up having to ride the bus from school or walk home. I'd be okay with walking, except Honeyton's winters are supposed to be intense, and riding the bus isn't fun at all, let alone for friendless people.

"I'll look into it," Aunt Beth assures her.

"You better." Dixie May frowns at the school. "Great. I bet there's not even any FHs here."

I roll my eyes. FHs stand for *fuckable hotties* in Dixie May language.

"Oh, I'm sure there are." My aunt smiles as she points at a muscular guy walking past our car. "Look at him. He's cute."

"Ew, Mom, you're so disgusting. Seriously, are you having a mid-life crisis or something?" Dixie May says with her nose crinkled. Then she sticks out one hand in her mom's direction while pulling the visor down. "Give me some lunch money, so I can get out of here and away from your gross comments."

"Oh, okay." My aunt starts rummaging through her purse.

While Dixie May waits for her mom to dig out some money, she does a quick check of her hair and makeup. She fixes a couple of her blonde curls, twisting them before flipping up the visor. Then she glances down at the pink top and white skirt she's wearing, smoothing out a few invisible wrinkles. By the time she's finished, Aunt Beth has put a twenty-dollar bill into her palm.

Dixie May stuffs it into her bag then shoves the door open and moves to get out, but then she pauses, glancing over her shoulder at me. "Don't even think about talking to me today. You know what will happen if you do."

"You'll have to pull out a dictionary to look up all the above four-letter words I'll use?" I question.

"Ravenlee," my aunt snaps, "don't be a brat."

"Yeah, Ravenlee, don't be a brat, or else everyone here is going to find out who you really are," Dixie May sneers with a smirk.

The muscles in my jaw tick, and I curl my fingers inward, stabbing my fingernails into my flesh and wrestling back the urge to punch that smirk off her face.

"Yeah, that's what I thought." Dixie May smirks at me one more time before climbing out of the car.

"Have a nice day," my aunt says to Dixie May, who shoves the door closed without even replying.

My aunt lets out a quiet sigh as Dixie May walks away, heading for the entrance doors. Once she's inside, Aunt Beth looks away, frowning at the passenger seat. "Crap, she forgot her makeup case." She reaches over, picks up a sparkly case, and hands it to me. "Find Dixie May and give this to her. And don't even think about stealing it. I'm going to text her to let her know you have it."

"She doesn't want me to talk to her, remember?" Not that I'm actually going to obey Dixie May. I really just don't want to talk to her or carry around her stupid sparkly case.

"I'm sure it'll be fine if you're giving her the case," she insists. When I make no effort to take it, she gives me a dirty look. "She needs her makeup, and you're going to take it to her because, unlike you, my daughter cares about her appearance."

"So what if I don't care?" I stuff the case into my bag. "Looking pretty isn't the most important thing in the world."

She arches a brow. "Have you looked in the mirror lately? You look like a homeless person."

Sometimes, I think she treats me so shitty because of how her husband and daughter treat her, like she's deflecting all her bottled-up aggravation on me. It used to hurt. Now it just pisses me off and makes me want to annoy her.

"Yeah, well, it's better than looking like a skank," I tell her.

Her eyes widen in horror. "My daughter does not look like a skank. How dare you say so?"

I raise a brow at her. "Who said I was talking about your daughter?"

She shakes her head furiously. "You know what? It's time for you to get out of this car. I'm sick of looking at you."

I'm more than ready to get out, but as I peer outside at the school, a drop of anxiety rises inside me.

Dixie May was right. It's a really small school. Way smaller than the one we used to go to. I don't know whether to be nervous about that or not. On the one hand, it means fewer people will mock me. But it also means people will be nosier.

"Get out!" Aunt Beth snaps. "And I'm not giving you any lunch money. You'll have to use your own."

"I'm not stupid enough to believe otherwise." I reach for the door handle.

Her lips curl into a sneer. "That's very debatable."

I push open the door. "So is Dixie May's IQ."

"Dixie May isn't stupid." She rotates around in the seat to glare at me. "She just prefers fashion and guys over schoolwork. That's not that uncommon for a teenage girl. You're the anomaly, Raven."

I give a shrug. "I wasn't trying to argue that I wasn't an anomaly. I was merely pointing out that, if you think I'm unintelligent, then you must think your daughter is an idiot."

"Dixie May isn't an idiot," she scoffs. "She just gets distracted because she has a life." She flashes me a smirk. "Unlike you."

"I may be a social outcast, but at least I'm not an idiot. And when this last year of hell is all over and I graduate, I'm going to take my good grades, go off to college, and make something of myself, while Dixie May probably ends up having a shotgun wedding because she can't keep her legs closed."

Her nostrils flare. "You little shit—"

I hop out of the car and slam the door shut.

She starts to roll the window down as I hurry toward the sidewalk that leads to the front doors, knowing she won't make a scene. It's not her style. No, her style is to tell my uncle, who's going to either be annoyed with her that she's being a tattletale or pissed off at me, depending on his mood. Either way, there's going to be shouting in the house when my uncle Don gets home tonight.

"You can get your own ass home, Ravenlee Wilowwynter!" she shouts from the car. "I won't be picking you up!"

I cringe as the handful of students walking around glance in my direction.

Awesome. What a great way to start my first day at a new school. Then again, if Dixie May has her way, it'll be a shitty day for me anyway. And now I have the walk home to look forward to. It's my own damn fault for riling my aunt up. I just get so sick of her shit sometimes.

Letting out a slow exhale, I continue toward the school with people eyeballing me, eyeballing my outfit, eyeballing my crazy hair. Then the whispering begins. Finally, I can't take it anymore, so I stick my hand into my pocket and dig out my phone. Then I grab my earbuds, pop them in, and crank up some classic rock, the same music my dad used to listen to.

I've been entering school this way for as long as I can remember. Music helps block out everything, including my own annoying thoughts. Though I made a promise to myself not to do that today, to try a fresh start, I guess old habits die hard.

I don't want to listen to the whispering. Don't want to listen to the name calling. Don't want to listen to everyone talk about all the made-up stories Dixie May has spread about me.

"She's a slut."

"She's a satanic freak."

"I once saw her kill a puppy just for fun."

"She slept with a teacher."

"Slut."

"Freak."

"Murderer."

I yank myself away from the memories, telling myself that I don't need to rehash the lies she told about me.

Well, almost all of them were lies.

One carries a drop of truth to it.

Murderer.

Because, in a way, their deaths were my fault.

3

HUNTER

I'm having the shittiest morning ever, mostly because one of the first people I see is my stepmother from hell. I despise the woman. Hate her. Just seeing her makes my skin crawl, which is why I try to avoid her at all costs.

I don't live with her or my father, having rented a house with my two best friends, Jax and Zay, the day I turned eighteen. We made a pact to do so when we were twelve, to move away from the shitholes that were supposed to be our homes but, really, were just houses, with roofs and walls that offered shelter. Nothing more. And yeah, I know that's more than what some people have.

The houses are huge, too, since all our parents are pretty wealthy. So, most everyone who doesn't really know us, which is honestly everyone outside our group, thinks of us as spoiled brats. They don't know all the ugliness that's gone on in our homes. Of how we were broken. Of how our parents—if you can even call them that—got that wealth that they flash around for the entire town to see.

Money and power. That's all our families care about. And that kind of mentality makes people do messed-up stuff, makes them cold and uncaring.

But Jax, Zay, and I left all that behind the start of our senior year when we moved out of our homes and into our own place and started our own business. Our parents weren't happy at all, mostly because it made them look bad, as if their children didn't want to be part of the family anymore. Which is completely true. And if I'm being honest, what happened this morning is exactly what I've been expecting to happen since the day we moved out.

It started with my wicked wench of a stepmom knocking on the front door of our two-story home in the small neighborhood we live in. While the place isn't a dump, it's also nowhere near close to the mansion I grew up in, which is what I wanted—to remain lowkey and live a normal life. Well, for the most part. Our job choice is anything but normal. But hardly anyone knows about what we do.

The Raven Three. That's what we call our company. And our job business description includes hacking, digging up intel, tracking someone down, and pretty much anything that has to do with solving a mystery for someone. We're basically a private investigative business, although we don't call ourselves that. We learned all our skills from the best, too, since my father has several private investigators on hand for his business. Having grown up around it, we got to learn the trade, and now we use it to our benefit. We have to remain anonymous as possible, though, which we do.

Creating the business allowed us to move out of the house and gave us a chance at attempting to live a semi-normal life, minus the whole PI thing. But I should've known better. You can't be a Hathingford and live a normal life. No, in order to be one, you have to be corrupt —it's how my family got and kept their wealth and status. And everyone with the last name has to play their part, something I am reminded of when I step out onto the front porch of my home.

She didn't even knock, which causes me to startle.

"Holy shit," I breathe out with my hand pressed to my chest as I stumble back.

Once I see who it is, I start to turn to go back in the house where I plan on locking the door and staying in there until she leaves.

"I wouldn't do that if I were you," she tells me with a warning tone. "Unless you want this," she pauses, her tone oozing with sarcasm as she eyeballs the house, "lovely little set up of yours to be over." She grins as I grit my teeth and stay put.

A few of my neighbors are wandering around and eyeballing the scene. I don't blame them. On top of her shiny red Porsche parked out front, she's wearing a red dress, a leather jacket, and a diamond necklace. If I didn't know better, I'd guess she was going out clubbing, but this is how she always looks—overly dressed with sparkly things decorating her. She's kind of a sparkly thing herself, being about fifteen years younger than my father. The only reason she married him was for his money and power. She doesn't love him, doesn't care that he sleeps around, doesn't care about anything except what she wants. And she'll do anything to get it.

Anything.

"Smart boy," she says, her grin broadening, her gaze trailing over me.

I hate when she looks at me. I often dream about a day when I can gouge out her eyes so she can never look at anyone again. But my father has made a rule that she's off limits, and if I break any of my father's rules while I'm still living in town, Jax, Zay, and I will be punished for it. I know it sounds crazy, but trust me, that's how much power my father has over this town. And me.

"What do you want?" I bite out, crossing my arms and leaning against the doorframe, trying to appear more confident than I really am.

She doesn't answer right away, just smiles at me, toying with me—her favorite thing to do.

She once told me I was her favorite toy, but it never really made any sense, since she did everything in her power to break me.

But I didn't break. I'm still standing here. Granted, I wish she wasn't here.

"One of your father's employees has bailed out," she informs me.

By bailed out, she means either he ran or is currently at the bottom of a lake somewhere.

I lift my brows at her. "So? What does that have to do with me?"

"He needs you and your little friends to fill in," she explains, fiddling with one of her earrings.

I promptly shake my head. "No way." I step back inside and move to shut the door, but she slams her palm against it.

"If you don't do this, he'll make your life a living hell. And you should know better than anyone that he can very well do that."

My fingers curl inward, my fingernails piercing my flesh. I want to scream out a protest, but know she's right. I hate how much I know she's right.

"I'll just do it," I tell her. "Zay and Jax don't need to get involved." Deep down, I know this is a pointless argument. Because Zay's father and Jax's father work with my dad so, more than likely, they've sent the wicked wench to deliver messages to their sons, too.

She rolls her eyes. "You know that's not how this is going to work. Their fathers have instructed that they be part of this, too." She smiles at me. "Your first job is tonight."

"What's the job?" I ask, not really wanting to hear the answer. But eventually, I'm going to have to, so I might as well rip off the Band-Aid.

"For now, you're going to be doing intel on the new sheriff," she explains, her heels clicking against the front porch as she backs away. "You're to find out what sort of guy he is then report back to me."

While it sounds easy enough, spying on the sheriff is never a good thing. Plus, if the dude turns out to be a good guy, my father will do everything in his power to ruin his life and get him fired. Because, if he can't be bought off, then my father can't continue running his illegal businesses that range from drug trafficking to illegal underground casinos. Yeah, he's a real winner.

I sometimes wonder if he was always like this, or if perhaps when my mom was alive, he was a different man. She died when I was two, so I don't remember the time she was alive, and my dad refuses to talk about that time. He won't even tell me stories about her, and he got rid of most of her stuff, except for a few photos. All I know is that she gave birth to me, had the same blonde hair as me, and died right after she gave birth to my younger sister, Harlow, who unfortunately still lives with my father, although she stays over here as much as she can.

"Stop by the diner after school and pick up the information on him. Text me when you're heading there so I don't have to wait around, but be vague about your word choice—don't use anything incriminating. And don't be too late. I have a salon appointment later." She continues to back away, lifting her hand and waggling her fingers at me. Then her gaze drifts to something over my shoulder and the corners of her lips tug downward.

"What the hell are you doing here?" Jax's voice sails over my shoulder as he steps up beside me.

I feel a bit better having him there, and I hate that I'm that way. Hate that I'm a coward when it comes to Diane. Plus, Jax can be a scary mothereffer when he wants to be. He's a softy at heart, though he'd try to kick my ass if I ever told anyone that. I never would. My friends and I have worked hard at creating the façade that we portray to everyone else outside of our circle. We're only who we really are when we're only around each other. To everyone else, we appear cold, collected, and in control of everything. It's the best way to not get screwed over, which happens a lot when you come from wealthy, powerful families. Jax, Zay and I learned from a young age that people will use us if we let them. We don't. Not anymore.

"I came here to give you details on a job you've been assigned to," Diane tells him. "Hunter can inform you."

Unlike with me, she doesn't toy with Jax, turning away and hurrying toward her car.

"Please tell me she's kidding," Zay says as he steps up beside Jax.

I sigh heavily as I step outside to head to school, like I was planning to before I ran into the wicked witch. "Unfortunately, she's not. At least the job doesn't sound *too* awful."

Jax's cocks a brow as he walks out behind me. "Anything that has to do with our fathers is bad. Besides, we have our own jobs we need to take care of."

"I know," I mutter, dragging my fingers through my hair and sighing.

Zay sighs, too, as he walks out and shuts the front door behind him. "What's the job?"

"We're supposed to get intel on the new sheriff," I explain as I dig the keys to my baby blue 1969 Camaro out of my pocket.

"There's a new sheriff?" Zay asks as he locks the front door and pockets the keys.

I shrug. "Apparently."

"So, we're basically finding out if he's corrupt," Jax states, slipping on a pair of sunglasses

I nod as I make my way to the driveway. "Pretty much."

"That doesn't sound too bad, then," Jax states as we reach the car. "Well, unless he's some sort of saint."

"Yeah," I agree, crossing my fingers he's not.

Otherwise, the information we gather on him might be the start of his death certificate.

4

RAVEN

I DECIDE to take a little detour before I enter the school and sneak out by the dumpsters to take a few hits. It's a risky move, for sure, since I'm not familiar with how this school works, but I need my *calm*.

I smoke until my mind is hazy. I smoke until I can't feel anything but sedation, numbness. I smoke until I can't think about much of anything.

Emptiness. Just how I like it.

Once I'm good and blazed, I spray some perfume on, put some eye drops in, and then head inside the school.

Last night, my aunt told me that I'm supposed to stop by the office this morning to pick up my schedule. I expect to see Dixie May in there and plan on giving her the stupid, sparkly case then, but by the time I enter the office, she's either already picked up her schedule, or she decided to spend the morning trying to find a clique she can dictate.

The secretary sitting behind the front desk looks up at me as I wander in, eyeing my outfit. After seeing how most of the people in the hallway are dressed, I kind of expected that.

Preppy is the word that came to mind when I noted the outfits almost everyone is sporting. Not that I believe everyone is preppy here, but there are an awful lot of Polo shirts and khakis.

Once the secretary is done scrutinizing me, her lips move, but I can't hear what she's saying.

Shit. I forgot I had my earbuds in.

I tug one out. "Sorry, I didn't hear you. Can you repeat that?"

She gives me a wary look, and I wonder if she suspects I'm high as a mothereffer.

"I said, can I help you with something?" she asks with mild tolerance.

I do my best to focus on her and rest my arms on the counter. "Yeah, I'm new here and need to get my schedule."

She turns toward the computer. "What's the name?"

"Ravenlee Wilowwynter."

She starts typing then pauses. "How do you spell the last name?"

I spell it for her, and she types it in, briefly smiling. "That's a beautiful name. Does it mean anything?"

I could tell her the reason my parents named me after the cursed bird, tell her the prettier part of the name, but nothing about me or my life is pretty anymore, so I answer her with honesty instead. "Yeah, bad luck. Or, well, Raven does, which is what I go by, so ..."

She glances up at me with her brows furrowed. "Excuse me?"

"Raven, the bird, represents bad luck," I say with a shrug. "Which is what people call me."

She blinks. "Oh." Then she starts to look back at her computer.

Awesome, Raven. She definitely probably thinks you're on something.

I'd probably be more worried, but that numbness I love so much has settled me.

Calms me.

Calm.

"They also symbolize wisdom, knowledge, creativity, mysteriousness, and unpredictability," a guy who looks to be around my age says as he steps up beside me.

I start to turn my head, wondering how the hell this guy knows what ravens symbolize, and then I blink, sure I'm seeing things.

He seriously might be the prettiest guy I've ever seen, with chin-length blond hair, long eyelashes, and bright blue eyes. And just by looking at his pretty face, I expect him to be dressed in an outfit that goes with the preppy theme around here. So, I'm surprised he's wearing a black shirt, matching jeans, and boots. He also has a chain dangling from his belt loop and leather bands covering his wrists.

The strangest part about him is the way he's smiling at me. I can't even remember the last time someone smiled at me, let alone some pretty guy with eyelashes so long I swear he could be wearing mascara.

"Are you real?" I ask, blinking again.

His forehead creases, yet the corners of his lips quirk. "Yeah. Are you?"

I nod, pulling my head out of my ass.

Did I just ask this guy if he's real?

Dude, I smoked way too much this morning.

"Good morning, Mr. Hathingford," the secretary greets him with what can only be described as a somewhat tolerant, somewhat amused look. Still, the look lets me know this pretty guy is totally real. "And to what do I owe the pleasure of your presence today?"

He rests his arms on the counter and gives her the same charming smile he tried to dazzle me with. "Now, what'd be the fun in just telling you? Let's make a game out of it. I'll give you three tries to guess, and if you guess wrong, I get to walk out of here, free and clear."

I glance at the secretary, expecting her to get annoyed.

Instead, she shakes her head and cracks a small smile. "I'm not going to guess, because I already know. And I'll give you the pass for today. This is the last time, though. I swear, the next time you come and ask me for one, I'm going to give you a detention slip instead." Then she pushes back from the desk, stands up, and walks off toward the back of the room.

Grinning, the guy leans over the counter, steals a sucker out of a bin on her desk, and then pops it into his mouth.

Okay, I guess it's going to take a while to get my schedule.

I start to lift my earbud toward my ear, preparing to go back to my Zen state, when the guy smiles at me.

"So, girl who's most definitely real, are you new here?" he asks, rolling the sucker in his mouth. "I haven't seen you around."

I could just answer him—it'd be the polite thing to do. I could try to be nice and see if I can make a friend, but that'd be pretty naïve of me. And while I may be a lot of things, I'm not polite nor naïve. So, I let out a quiet sigh and lower my earbud. "Do I really need to answer that?"

Amusement sparkles in his eyes as he angles his head to the side in confusion. "Yeah ... Why wouldn't you? I mean, I did answer you when you asked me if I was real."

True, but still...

I cross my arms on top of the counter. "Yeah, but this

school has a total of what? Like two hundred people? So I'm pretty confident you know you've never seen me around before and already know I'm new."

His confusion fades, amusement taking over. He pulls the sucker out of his mouth. "That's an excellent point." He gives a glance around before leaning toward me. "Want to know a little secret? I really did know you are new. I was just trying to find an opening to start a conversation with you."

I struggle not to smile. "As flattered as I am, I can totally assure you that, come lunchtime, you're going to pretend like I'm invisible."

His amused smile remains, but his brows pull together. "And why's that?"

"Because you're an FH," I reply with a half-shrug.

His amusement doubles. "Do I want to know what that stands for?"

I shrug. "I'm sure you'll figure it out eventually."

His grin widens. "Maybe you should just tell me now and spare me the headache I always get when I think too much. And while we're at it, why don't you tell me something about you? Like, what grade you're in, where you moved from, if you have a boyfriend ..."

Wait ... Is he flirting with me?

It's not like I've never had a guy flirt with me before. I have a couple of times, but it usually happened at school, and Dixie May always found a way to ruin whatever allure I had toward the few guys who gave me more than a second glance. And, while I'm totally flattered that the prettiest guy that I've ever seen is semi-flirting with me, I know that, when Dixie May spots him, he won't ever smile at me again. Because she *will* spot him. The guy is way too pretty for her not to notice. And, while style-wise, the two of them don't look similar, their pretty faces will go well together on those shotgun wedding invitations.

"Nah, I'd rather not," I tell him, figuring he'll back off, but he only grows more intrigued.

"Oh, come on; just a little bit of information. That's all I'm asking."

"Nah. I think I'm going to hold on to my mysteriousness for now. Make sure I'm representing the symbolism of my name to its truest form."

He chuckles softly. "Hate to break it to you, but you already messed up with that, because you just gave me a little bit of info about yourself."

"Um, no, I didn't."

"Yes, you did."

"How?"

He grins, pointing the sucker at me. "You let me know you're amusing."

"Oh, I'm not," I assure him. "I'm being totally serious."

"I have no doubt you are, but it's still amusing." He

gives a short, considering pause. "And I also think you're a little bit stubborn."

I roll my eyes. "You can't determine that after talking to me for, like, thirty seconds."

He throws a dramatic glance at the clock. "Actually, it's been a little over a minute."

"That's still not enough time."

"Says who?"

"Says the person who determined the time length required to be able to give an accurate analysis of someone's character."

He cocks a brow. "And what's this person's name? Because, as far as I know, no one has ever come up with such a thing."

"His name is Jerry." I make up a name then decide to make up a story. "And he lives somewhere in Switzerland where there's no internet or cell service, so he hasn't been able to publish his findings yet. But I met him once while I was on vacation, and me and Jerry had a good, long chat about his theory on the time it takes to get to know a person. And he told me that you have to know someone a lot longer than a minute to determine what kind of person they are."

He stares at me confoundedly, and I wait for him to back off, to realize I'm a weirdo that he doesn't want to know. Instead, a grin takes over his face.

"You and I have to be friends," he insists.

I shake my head. "Sorry, but that can't happen."

"Why not?" He sulks, jutting out his lip, pouting. He looks adorable when he does it and seems like the kind of guy who knows it.

"Because it just won't work." Again, I struggle not to smile, but I'm totally gonna blame it on being buzzed.

He shakes his head then grins. "I think it totally will. In fact, I think we might be the perfect match."

"Trust me; I know it won't work." *Because Dixie May will make sure of it, even if she has to tell you about how I might be a murderer.*

"There's no way you can possibly know that." He gives me a curious look. "Unless you're a psychic."

"As awesome as that would be, I'm just a normal girl," I assure him, tucking a strand of hair behind my ear.

He stares at me in a way that makes me squirm. "I really doubt that. In fact, I think you might be one of the most interesting people I've met in a long time."

I tug at the sleeve of my jacket, a self-conscious move I always do to make sure my scars are hidden. "Do I really need to tell you again about Jerry and his theory?"

"Yes, *theory*," he stresses. "Not fact."

"Did I say theory?" I smack the heel of my hand to my forehead. "I meant fact. Stupid me, I always get the two mixed up."

His grin is as shiny as a goddamn black diamond ring

and just as pretty. "Yeah, we're definitely going to be friends."

I'm racking my brain for a good protest when the secretary returns with a pink slip of paper in her hand. She smiles as she hands the paper to the guy. "This will get you out of last period, and last period only, which I noted multiple times on the slip. And in permanent marker," she warns. "Do not try to pull any of that funny business like you did last time when you erased the date and gave it to all your teachers to get out of all your classes."

He presses his hand to his chest and dazzles her with a grin. "You have my word. No more funny business."

She sighs tiredly. "One of these days, I'm just going to tell you no."

"But today's not that day." He winks at her.

The bell rings then, announcing class is about to start and that I was right when I guessed I was going to be late.

"Just get to class," she tells him then sinks down into her chair.

He salutes her then turns to me. "I'll see you around, mysterious Raven. And when I do, I expect some more details about you. You know, so we can start establishing our beautiful, impending friendship." He winks at me then pops the sucker into his mouth and strolls out of the office.

"That one is a handful," the secretary remarks as she types a few things onto her computer.

I focus on her. "Yeah, I can tell."

She clicks the mouse. "He's a good kid, though, especially considering what he's been through. It's also probably why I have a hard time telling him no."

I want to ask her so many questions, like why she gave him a slip to get out of class, or what he's been through or, better yet, what his name is since all I ever heard her call him was Mr. Hathingford. But doing so would mean I have an interest in him and would put me a little bit closer to knowing who he is. What would be the point in that?

Like I said before, by the end of the day, he'll have no desire to be friends with me anymore.

5

HUNTER

So maybe this day isn't going to be as shitty as I thought. Sure, I still have to do that job for my dad, and school isn't my favorite place ever, but basketball is starting up today, which I'm on the team. Planning offers me a couple of hours of peace from the chaos that is my life.

That's not the only thing that's gotten my mood elevating. It's the new girl. I'm going to call it total luck that I met her in the main office on the start of her first day. Although, according to her, she'd probably call it bad luck.

She's amusing, she really is, and freakin' gorgeous. That was the first thing I noticed when I walked into the main office to get a pass to miss last period so I can have time to meet Diane at the diner and still make it back to practice.

That long, wavy hair that reminded me of the color of raven feathers, those long legs and that ass ... It was a really nice view. But nothing compared to when she turned and looked at me. Those eyes, those beautiful hazel eyes that carry so much pain in them. I could see it. This girl had been hurt by something or someone. And in those eyes, I saw a bit of familiarity, probably because the hurt looks so similar to what's in my own eyes and my friends'.

And, being me, I flirted with her. It's what I'm known for. But usually, it's just an act.

This ... This felt real.

I *wanted* to flirt with her.

What made it even more amusing is that she seemed completely unimpressed by my charm. That was definitely a first.

By the time I exited the office, I'm sure I had a dumbass grin on my face.

"Dude, what're you smiling about?" my younger sister, Harlow, asks as I near my locker where she's waiting for me.

She looks similar to me—blonde hair, blue eyes. When we were younger, she used to wear dresses all the time and curl her hair. Around the end of middle school, though, she decided to reinvent herself for who the hell knows why. Now she wears a lot of torn jeans, black T-shirts, sneakers, and has a shit ton of piercings.

"There's this new girl—"

"Isn't there always?" she cuts me off with a roll of her eyes.

I give her a *hardy har* look. "Very funny."

She grins, leaning against the locker. "Fine. Tell me about this new girl."

"Well, she's new, like new to Honeyton," I explain as I spin the combination to my locker.

She crinkles her nose. "Oh God, please don't tell me that's her." She points down the hallway.

I turn and spot a blonde girl I've never seen before walking down the hallway. She's shimmying her hips and smiling like she's some sort of beauty queen on display.

"No, that's definitely not her." I open my locker.

"So, there's *another* new girl starting today?" Harlow remarks. "That's kind of weird."

She's right. Honeyton isn't very big, so we don't get a lot of new students.

"Maybe they're sisters."

"Doubtful." I grab my English book and close my locker.

Harlow arches her brow at me. "Why do you say that?"

"Because the girl I met earlier looks nothing like her." I nod my head at Beauty Queen.

"Siblings can be totally different," she reminds me. "Or they could be half-sisters. Or step-sisters."

"Yeah, maybe," I say as we start down the hallway. As the bell rings, I turn toward my classroom. "Did you need something? Or did you just do a locker stop to give me shit?"

"As much as I love giving you shit about stuff, I actually need a favor," she tells me, digging her phone out of her pocket. "I want to leave campus for lunch, but Dad made me use the driver to get to school today, so I'm wondering if I can borrow your car. I know you have to go meet your coach at lunch to sign some forms."

"How did you know that?"

She shrugs with a mischievously glint in her eyes. "Because I'm a mind reader." When I lift my brow in challenge, she dramatically sighs. "Fine. I overheard you talking about it yesterday. Way to take away my awesome façade at being a mind reader."

I shake my head but smile at her. "You're such a little weirdo."

"Hey, I'm far from little anymore, but I'll own my weirdo-ness," she tells me. "So, can this weirdo borrow your car?"

I waver. On the one hand, I really love my car and rarely let anyone drive it. On the other hand, I really love my sister and have always tried to be a good big brother, despite how complicated she makes that sometimes.

"Fine. Just be safe, okay?" I take my keys out and give them to her.

She grins as she takes them. "Thanks. You're the best big brother ever."

No, I'm not. I'll only earn that title the day I find a way to get her out of my father's house. Until then, I'm completely and utterly failing.

6

RAVEN

Like I guessed, I end up having to walk into first period late. Thankfully, the teacher lets me slide on in without too much of a fuss. And as a double bonus, Dixie May isn't in this class.

I keep waiting for something to happen. For the whispering to start. For the labels to begin being thrown at me. Strangely, the morning goes by pretty uneventfully. Well, until fourth period rolls around.

Like I did in every other one of my classes, I first go talk to the teacher when I walk in to tell him that I'm new.

"Oh, yes, right." Mr. Mcnellton, a middle-aged guy with thinning hair, glances up from the stack of papers on his desk. "I think your sister was in my second period class."

"Cousin," I correct. "But, yeah, we live together."

"Oh, I see." He clearly doesn't, confusion flooding his eyes.

He wants to ask questions, but like most, he won't, over the fear that the answer might be uncomfortable to hear.

It is, too, for everyone who dares to ask.

The girl who possibly murdered her parents.

He clears his throat then adjusts his tie. "Well, you can sit anywhere you like. The seats aren't assigned. And I'm sure I'm going to enjoy having you in my class."

I want to tell him my story of Jerry and his theory that proves there's no way he can be sure of that, but I decide to attempt to keep on the teacher's good side for now. So, I simply nod then wander toward a row of desks lining the middle of the classroom, choosing the far back one where I can keep my head low and hopefully not get called on.

Once I'm seated, I set my binder on the desk, pop my earbuds in, and then recline back in the seat. I have about four minutes until the bell rings, so I should be able to listen to one full song.

A minute later, I'm zoned out, tapping my fingers to the beat, when a guy approaches my desk. He has on a black hoodie with the hood drawn over his head, and his eyes are as dark as storm clouds, although completely and utterly gorgeous—and intense. His jawline is covered with stubble, along with a scar, and his expression is intense. I'm not sure what he wants, but I don't really care too much, at least not enough to take my earbuds out. He makes no effort to move, though, continuing to stare at me.

What the hell is this guy's deal?

I tug one of my earbuds out. "Can I help you?"

"Yeah, you're in my seat," he grumbles.

I'm so confused. "Really? Because the teacher said they aren't assigned."

A beat of silence passes by as he stares at me intimidatingly.

"They're not officially assigned," he finally states with a hint of annoyance. "But anyone who has any self-preservation knows not to sit in that seat." He nods at the desk on my right then my left. "Or in those."

I tap my finger against my lip. "Huh. I guess I must've left my self-preservation at home today."

The tiniest bit of surprise flickers in his eyes, but he swiftly extinguishes it. "Well, I suggest you go find it before you end up doing something stupid." He places his hands on my desk and leans in. "Now get out of my seat."

My heart thunders in my chest. How do I want to handle the situation? I mean, I want to keep going about my day unnoticed, and if I put up a fight with this guy, that'll draw attention. But his demanding attitude is annoying. It's like he just expects me to do what he says, like everyone in this world does.

He's like a male version of Dixie May, only more intense.

His irritation festers the longer I sit in the seat without moving. His jaw ticks, his eyes darken, and his muscles wind into tight knots.

"Trust me, new girl; you really don't want to play this game with me," he warns in a low tone.

"What game?" I carry his gaze. "I'm just sitting at a desk, trying to mind my own business."

"At *my* desk," he stresses. "Now get up and go find a seat somewhere else before I make you."

My pulse spikes, but so does my stubbornness. When I was younger, my mom used to tell me that being stubborn would be a benefit and a curse. But she was wrong. It's only been a curse. I wish I could get rid of it, but sometimes it creeps up on me without warning. Like when brooding guys get up in my face and threaten me.

Lifting a brow, I recline in the seat.

Surprise blazes in his eyes. It's like no one has ever defied him before. It makes me feel both proud of myself and a bit nervous. But I conceal the latter. I'm good at that—concealing my emotions. Have been for the last almost six years.

His jaw ticks as he straightens. "Fine, you wanna play this way, then let's play."

I hold my breath, waiting for him to jerk me out of the seat or something. Instead, he turns around and drops into the seat in front of me.

"You just destroyed your chances of making it here,

new girl," he warns, throwing me a dirty look from over his shoulder.

"Awesome. I didn't have a chance anyway." I move to put my earbud back in.

"Hey, Mr. M." The blond guy from the office this morning strolls into the classroom, smiling at the teacher.

The teacher glances up from the papers. "Hey, Hunter. Are you excited for tryouts?"

So his name is Hunter, and I'm guessing he plays some sort of sport.

I crinkle my nose. Jocks are usually the worst. At least, they were at my old school. But Hunter doesn't look like the jocks at my last school.

Maybe he plays chess or is in the math league.

A smile tugs at my lips at the amusing thought.

At that exact moment, Hunter glances in my direction. I'm sure I look like a freak with a stupid grin on my face.

A smile appears on his lips. "Hey—"

I stuff my earbud into my ear.

Shaking his head and grinning, he starts down the aisle, his grin quickly dissipating as his gaze settles on the guy in front of me. His gaze dances from me to the guy, then his lips move.

I'm curious what they're talking about, but I refuse to let the curiosity win. Then the song ends, and it's the last song on my playlist, leaving the noise in the classroom to creep into my ears. I start to turn on another song.

"So, she stole your seat?" Hunter says to the guy, his voice a mixture of confusion and amusement.

"For today. But she'll learn her place soon enough," the guy warns, fishing a pen out of his pocket.

I pause from selecting a song, deciding to eavesdrop.

Hunter casts a glance in my direction then looks back at the guy. "Did you at least tell her that she was sitting in your seat?"

"Yep." He restlessly taps the pen against the desk. "Apparently, the girl has no self-preservation."

"Aw, come on, Zay; give her a break. She's new." Hunter plops down in the desk across from the guy. "Remember how scary it was on your first day?"

The guy—Zay—lets out a hollow laugh. "I wasn't scared."

"Bullshit," Hunter teases. "You were six. All six-year-olds get scared about their first day of school. Even you." When Zay doesn't respond, worry flickers across Hunter's face, his lips parting. "I'm sorry, Zay. I wasn't thinking when I said that."

"It doesn't fucking matter," Zay mumbles. "None of this does."

They grow quiet, and Hunter continues to frown as he sneaks glances at Zay. I can't tell if he's afraid of him or worried. Maybe a little of both. I find myself fascinated by it. How can he make people so afraid of him, even his own ... friend? If that's what Hunter is. What I wouldn't give to have that talent. Then maybe people would stop tormenting me.

Eventually, people begin pouring into the classroom. No one says anything to Hunter or Zay, but a lot of them do double-takes in their direction then gawk at me. I'm not positive, but I have a suspicion that it has to do with the new seating arrangement. Why the hell is it such a big deal? Just what kind of guy is Zay?

The frown remains on Hunter's face until a tall guy with dark, chin-length hair enters the room. Like Hunter, he's dressed all in black and has a pretty face, although his seems to have a more beautifully haunted way about him, all serious, as if he hasn't laughed in a very long time. He also has a lip and brow piercing and tattoos cover his lean arms.

"Dude," Hunter says as he approaches. "Why are you late?"

"I had to ..." He trails off as his gaze skates from Zay to me, a crinkle forming between his brows as he looks back at Hunter. "Did Mr. M. finally assign seats?"

Hunter shakes his head. "Nope."

The stranger looks at me, but I pretend not to notice, picking at my chipped fingernail polish.

He looks back at Hunter. "Is she aware she's sitting in Zay's seat?"

"Yeah," Hunter replies, leaning back in his seat and kicking his feet up onto the chair in front of him. "Apparently, she didn't want to move."

"She was a real bitch about it, too," Zay mumbles as he twists sideways in his seat.

So, I'm a bitch because I wouldn't move out of the seat when he demanded?

Annoyed, I tug out my earbuds. "I wasn't being a bitch just because I refused to obey you."

As Zay's gaze cuts to me, the stranger's brows rise while Hunter gives me some sort of cryptic pressing look.

Zay studies me for an intense beat. "You're right; you don't have any self-preservation."

"Actually, I think my exact words were I left it at home," I remind him. "Maybe I'll remember it tomorrow. But probably not since I have a habit of forgetting things. I'm so bad that I had to install that app on my phone that helps me find my phone because I keep losing it. But I don't think there's an app that helps people find their self-preservation. Maybe, though. I'll have to look into it."

Hunter smashes his lips together while the stranger stares at me with a crinkle between his brows.

Zay's dark gaze practically bores a hole into my head. "You know what? I think I'm going to enjoy teaching you your place here." Then he gets up and storms out of the classroom.

The stranger lets out an exhausted sigh. "Do you want to go check on him this time?" he asks Hunter.

Hunter shakes his head. "Might be better to let him vent it out this time."

"Maybe." The stranger drops into Zay's seat then turns around to look at me. "So, who are you?"

I have no plans of answering him, but Hunter does it for me.

"That'd be Ravenlee Wilowwynter. Raven for short." A smile dances at his lips as he glances at the stranger. "Ironic, isn't it?"

Huh?

The stranger stares at me with an unreadable expression. "Perhaps."

Dude, these guys are weird.

"I tried earlier to get more information out of her," Hunter informs him, still appearing amused, "but she insisted she wants to remain mysterious. I'll wear her down, though. In fact, I predict we're going to be BFFs by October eighth." He winks at me.

"That's a really random number," I tell him. "Maybe you're the psychic."

Strands of his hair fall into his eyes as he shakes his head. "Nah, I'm just a goal setter, something you should know about me if we're going to be friends. You should also know that I almost always meet my goals, so get ready to start making those friendship bracelets."

"You might want to go easy on setting that goal," the stranger warns, "until you talk to Zay."

What is Zay? Like their ringleader or something?

Hunter slumps back in his seat, totally sulking. "Jax, why you gotta always ruin my fun like that?"

"Someone has to be your babysitter," the stranger—Jax—tells him, digging his phone out of his pocket.

Hunter's pout deepens. "I don't need a babysitter. You just think I do."

Jax just rolls his eyes while opening a notebook.

The bell rings then and the teacher walks to the front of the classroom to start class.

Jax lowers his voice and whispers one final thing to Hunter. "Do I need to remind you of what happened with Clara? Or Jessa? Or Katy?" He gives Hunter a pressing look. "You get me? Or do you want me to keep jotting off names?"

Hunter frowns. "No, you can stop. I get it, and I'll try to back off." He flicks one quick glance in my direction, offering me what appears to be an apologetic look.

What the hell he's sorry for is beyond me. What I'd really like to know is what happened to those girls that Jax spoke of. And who the heck Jax, Zay, and Hunter are and why everyone appears to be afraid of them.

But, as a minute ticks by with me overanalyzing all sorts of ideas about it, I realize I'm focusing way too much time on these guys. And that's not my MO. So, I focus on class, refusing to even glance in Hunter's or Jax's direction.

But, for some strange reason, I swear Hunter is watching me. Why? I don't have a clue, but I'm worried this moment is going to come back and bite me in the ass.

7

RAVEN

Zay never returns to class. I hate that I'm aware of this. Just like I hate that I'm aware of how Hunter ignores me, even when we walk out of the classroom at almost the same time.

Apparently, the warning Jax gave Hunter was enough to make him back off his determination to become my new BFF. It's probably for the better since, pretty soon, he'll meet the spawn of Satan since it's lunchbreak, and then she'll inform him of the deaths I may have staining my hands.

"You're new, right?" A girl with long, brown hair and hazel eyes approaches me as I'm heading toward my locker. She's wearing jeans and a T-shirt, along with a plaid shirt and Converse sneaker. Her casual style makes her look like someone Dixie May wouldn't associate with, but I'm not going to discount the idea completely.

I nod, putting up my guard. "Yeah, I am."

She walks beside me, glancing behind us and down the hallway. Then she looks back at me and leans in. "Well, here's a little warning. That guy's seat you were sitting in today in class, his name is Zay and, trust me, you don't want to mess with him or his friends, Hunter and Jax, those other two guys that sat by you. They're kind of dangerous."

"Okay ...?" I'm bewildered. "Thanks for the warning and everything, but why is it such a big deal that I sat at this Zay dude's desk? I mean, the seats aren't assigned."

She wavers. "It's kind of hard to explain to an outsider, but I'll try to give you the quick version of the story. That way, you'll understand and hopefully make the smart choice of staying away from them."

I study her with suspicion. "Why would you do that? I mean, why are you helping me?"

"Because I was new once and had to learn the hard way." She smiles. "I'm Katy, by the way."

Katy. I heard Jax mention her name on that list he prattled off to Hunter. But, what happened to the girls on the list?

"I'm Raven," I tell her with a small smile.

It's weird smiling at school. It's been a long time.

A long damn time.

"Raven? Huh, I really like that name." She adjusts the handle of her backpack higher onto her shoulder. "It's way more original than Katy."

"I like Katy better," I tell her as I swing around a couple making out in the middle of the hallway.

"You must be crazy then," she jokes with a grin.

Man, if she only knew how close to the truth she was. How I briefly spent time in a psychiatric hospital right after my parents died.

"Maybe a little bit," I agree, my chest feeling slightly pressurized.

Slut.

Freak.

Murderer.

My scars throb.

She laughs like I'm making a joke, but I'm not. "You're funny, Raven. You should come sit with me and my friends at lunch." Her laughter fades and seriousness takes over. "It'll be good for you to have a group at this school, too. Someone to protect you."

Confusion swirls inside me. "Protect me from what?"

She sneaks a quick, nervous glance around at the people flooding the hallways. "The politics in this town. Sadly, the more money and power your family has here, the more shit you can get away with at this school. It's so bad that teachers will literally look the other way, even when someone is getting their ass kicked by some pretentious, rich, spoiled brat. And don't even get me started on the sexual assaults that get dusted under the rug."

Is she being serious? She sure looks like it, but ..."Doesn't anyone report that kind of stuff to the police?" I ask. "I mean, sexual assault cases don't really seem like they should be handled by school administrators."

"The police are just as bad at looking the other way, because they get bought off. And if they do try to do something about all the illegal crap going on in town, they end up like old Sheriff Bethrtor, may he rest in peace." She draws a cross over her chest. "Although, I heard a rumor that we have a new sheriff in town, so maybe that'll change. Doubtful, though."

Yeah, I doubt so, too, since my uncle isn't the type of do-gooder guy who will turn down cash to do the right thing. Obviously, since he has a huge-ass stash of stolen drugs. But I'm not about to tell her that.

"Yeah, maybe," I mumble.

She bobs her head up and down, dazing off for a minute. "But yeah, anyway, if you want to be smart and stay off the radar from all this corrupt shit, I'd recommend staying as far away from Zay, Jax, and Hunter as you can." She steps closer and lowers her voice. "Jax comes from one of the wealthiest families in town, and Zay is his cousin and lives with him. No one knows why he lives with him, but he's just as spoiled as Jax. I've heard rumors that his dad's straight-up crazy. And Jax's dad is a total asshole. He owns a huge part of the town, so a lot of people have to do what he says. It's really weird."

I attempt to process the information she just gave me but, *holy crap*, this is weird. "Well, what about Hunter?"

She goes all doe-eyed for a moment before hastily blinking away the look. "Hunter lives with Jax and Zay, too. His dad works for Jax's dad as his"—she makes air quotes—" 'business consultant.' But everyone around here is pretty sure he basically makes sure anything ugly that could potentially tarnish the Capperellie name gets wiped clean."

That sounds ... sketchy. "Wiped clean how?"

"I'm not sure, but there're a few theories. One being ..." She drags her finger across her throat. "So, yeah, if I were you, I'd stay away from them. Especially Hunter."

Does she really believe that? That Hunter's dad kills people? Or does she just like to spread rumors?

"Really? Because Zay seems scarier."

"Oh, Zay is completely scary," she assures me. "He's also into some really weird shit."

I adjust the books in my hand as we near my locker. "What kind of weird shit?"

She lifts a brow. "What sort of weird stuff do you think I'm talking about?"

I shrug. "I don't know."

She gives me a look like I'm an idiot. "Sexual shit."

"Oh." Now this is a topic of conversation I'm a bit

unfamiliar with, being a virgin and all. Not that I'm some sort of prude who's going to blush over this or something. And it's not like I'm saving myself for marriage or anything like that. I've just never had the opportunity to have sex. I've never even been out on a date. I did get kissed once, but it was a stolen kiss that I refuse to ever think about.

"I'm not positive how true the rumors are since I haven't, and never will, go near Zay," Katy continues, "but I've heard he's into some really twisted stuff. And he never kisses anyone on the mouth and rarely touches anyone when he's messing around with them. And I've heard he likes it rough."

Okay, I may be a little naïve when it comes to sexual stuff, but that seems a bit weird to me.

"Why's he like that?" I wonder, telling myself I'm only curious, not interested. Well, it might be a little bit of both.

She shrugs. "Who the hell knows? I've heard, like, a ton of rumors about it, but the only people who really know the truth are Zay, Hunter, and Jax."

"They're like best friends, right?" I stop in front of my locker and start to spin the combination.

"No. They're more than that," she tells me. When she notices the confusion on my face, she adds, "It's kind of hard to explain, but the three of them are like some sort of freaky, human wolf pack or something. When I first moved here, I thought they were brothers, but I quickly learned their relationship is tighter than that. They aren't friends with anyone else, they never bring in outsiders, and they make no effort to associate with anyone, yet they always get invited to every party. It's partially out of fear and partially because I think a lot of people are hoping they'll be the lucky asshole who gets brought into their group." She shakes her head with a disgusted look on her face. "I don't know why they consider it lucky, though. They're jerks. And crazy. And just ..." She shakes her head again.

"Sounds like you got a beef with them," I say as I pull open my locker.

She chews on her bottom lip. "Well, I hooked up with Hunter once. It was the biggest mistake of my life, something I realized right after, when he told me to take care and left me lying in bed naked. He didn't even wait for me to get dressed before ditching me. And we were at his house, and he just took off, and ..." She clears her throat. "Anyway, I should've known better, because that's what Hunter does. He uses girls and everyone knows this, yet I somehow convinced myself that I'd be the one to change him."

"I'm sorry ... I can kind of see how you fell for him, though. He seems really ..." I waver for the right word. "Charming."

"You've talked to him?" she asks, and for the strangest second, I detect a hint of jealousy in her eyes.

I nod, my guard going up even more. If she is jealous, then that means she's not over him, and I don't need any jealous girl drama on top of the drama Dixie May is going to cause for me.

"Yeah, he was in the main office this morning when I picked up my schedule." I choose my words carefully. "He just said hi, but I wasn't really that interested in him."

Her brows elevate. "Seriously?"

"Yep."

"How? I mean, you did see him, right?"

I nod. "Yeah."

She gapes at me. "And you didn't think he was hot?"

"No." Not a total lie. Yeah, I thought he was pretty, but I'm not about to tell her that aloud.

She shakes her head, her jaw practically hanging to her knees. "You really are crazy, aren't you?"

I bump my locker shut. "I think we already established that, didn't we?"

Grinning, she points a finger at me. "You know what? I think you and I are going to be good friends."

That's the second time someone has said that to me today, but that doesn't mean I'm hopeful. No, I've had friends before. However, they ended the moment my parents died. For anyone else who thought to be my friend, they quickly reconsidered after they found out the truth. And I know it'll always be that way, because no one wants to be friends with a murderer.

Her lips part then close, her forehead creasing as she retrieves her phone from her pocket. She reads a message then curses. "Shit. I forgot I was supposed to meet the counselor at lunchtime." She stuffs her phone into her pocket. "I gotta go, but if you want, you can sit by my friends at lunch. They sit at the table near the far back doors." She backs away from me, moving down the hallway. "Most of them will have sketchbooks out, 'cause we're all art nerds. But we're cool. I promise." She throws me a wave then spins around, her shoes squeaking against the linoleum as she hurries off.

Sighing, I wander down the hallway, trying to decide whether or not I want to endeavor to the cafeteria or just skip lunch and pick something up on the walk home waiting for me at the end of the day. Normally, I skip lunch, mostly because of an incident in seventh grade when I got a tray of spaghetti dumped onto my head, then everyone started cracking jokes about how I must've killed someone again, that the spaghetti sauce was really blood. After that, I made a point to bring my lunch and eat it in the bathroom. Then, eventually, I started walking to food places to get something to eat. But I don't know my way around town yet, so I'm unsure if I have time to make it to any fast food places in time.

I could take up Katy's offer and try to sit by her

friends, but without her around, it just seems weird. And who knows if rumors have been spreading about me yet? I haven't heard anything, so maybe Dixie May is waiting to spill the gossip about me. Why she's waiting, I have no damn clue.

And what about this Zay guy? He warned me that he was going to show me my place in this town. Before, I wasn't that worried, but after what Katy told me, I feel slightly apprehensive. I'd probably be scared shitless if I hadn't spent the last six years of my life living in bullied hell every day.

Slut.

Freak.

Murderer.

Just as I'm about to arrive at the cafeteria, I receive a text message, which is weird. No one ever texts me. Like ever. Well, except for on the rare occurrence when my aunt notifies me of a chore that she wants me to do while she's out. It's really the only reason I have a phone. And it's a really shitty phone. Like, I'm talking one that flips open.

I dig my phone out of my pocket, and my guard instantly goes up when I see Bitchy Bitch of the West has texted me. Aka, Dixie May.

Bitchy Bitch of the West: My mom says you have my makeup case. You better give it to me ASAP before I get pissed. And you better not

touch any of my makeup. The last thing I want is to get like herpes or something from you.

I roll my eyes as I type back.

Me: Yes, I have it. And no, I didn't touch it. I have no desire to look like Bobo the Clown on my first day of school.

Bitchy Bitch of the West: Nah, you just prefer to look like a hobo, which, FYI, you're doing a stellar job at.

Me: Well, at least I can do a stellar job at something. You can't even work your clown look.

Bitchy Bitch of the West: You know what? I was trying to be nice to you, but since you've decided to be such a bitch, I think I'm going to let everyone know who you really are. I've already obtained the phone numbers of some very popular people in the school, and I think I'm going to send them a link to that article about your parents' deaths.

I grit my teeth so hard my jaw aches.

Me: You can, but then I just might dump your makeup case in the trash.

Bitchy Bitch of the West: Don't be a freakin' idiot. There's like hundreds of

dollars' worth of makeup in that case. And the case is designer!

Me: Yeah, so? Like you've pointed out a ton of times, I don't really care about that sort of stuff.

Bitchy Bitch of the West: Raven, I swear to God, if you don't give me my makeup case, I'm gonna make your life a living hell.

Like she isn't already going to do that.

Me: Fine. Where do you want to meet up so I can give it to you?

Bitchy Bitch of the West: We can meet up after lunch by the dumpsters out back where no one will see us together.

I roll my eyes, but type *okay* and stuff my phone back into my pocket. Then I debate what to do, whether I should go eat in the cafeteria with Katy and her friends or not. It sounds good in theory, but I can't stop thinking about all the times I got trays of food dumped onto my head by Dixie May's minions.

"If I were you, I'd stay away from her," a voice creeps from the shadows of a nearby alcove. Moments later, a girl steps out from it. She has long, blonde hair, blue eyes, and is sporting torn black jeans, a baggy T-shirt, and knee-high Converse sneakers.

"Stay away from who?" I ask, completely confused.

She points up the hallway. "Katy Kiss-ass."

"You mean the girl I was talking to a few minutes ago? Why? She seemed nice enough." Nicer than most people.

She snorts a laugh. "Trust me; she's not nice at all. And all that shit she just said about my brother and his friends isn't true. She just likes to gossip." She frowns as she mumbles, "Just like almost everyone else in this damn school."

"Wait ... who's your brother?" I ask, knowing she means either Jax, Zay, or Hunter, since that's who Katy was talking about. Before she can answer, though, I note her blonde hair and blue eyes, and it clicks. "Never mind. You have to be Hunter's sister, right?"

"So you've met my brother?" she asks, stepping closer to me.

I nod. "Yeah, for a few minutes in the main office this morning. And then I had fourth period with him." I don't bother mentioning the crapfest that happened between Hunter, his friends, and me.

"Oh." Her eyes light up with recognition, which puzzles the heck out of me. "You're the new girl."

I shift my weight. "Um, yeah. I'm Ravenlee. Or, well, Raven. No one really calls me Ravenlee."

She glances over me then chews on her bottom lip, as if she finds something hilarious.

I start to grow self-conscious and brace myself for some sort of rude remark about to be thrown my way.

"You know, something my brother said to me this

morning is totally making sense now," she remarks. Then she smiles. "I'm Harlow, by the way. I'm Hunter's little sister and the school's official outcast."

I arch a brow. "The school has an official outcast, huh? Wow, that's pretty impressive."

"Oh, it totally is," she quips. "I had to fill out a lot of paperwork to earn the title, along with having to endure a series of torture tests, which included but was not limited to mockery over my looks, who my family is and, most importantly, the fact that I don't have any friends."

"Sounds like you and I have a lot in common," I joke. "In fact, you might have yourself a little bit of a challenge for keeping your outcast title."

She grins. "Perhaps. I don't know, though ... You don't seem like you have your weirdo image down as well as I do." She gestures at my outfit.

I crack a small smile. "Dude, we're dressed very similar."

She taps her bottom lip. "Really? I don't see it."

I grin. So does she. And I realize that I think I might actually have a connection with this girl. Maybe we can even be friends?

Of course, that moment is completely shattered as some guy wearing a baseball cap strolls by, grinning at Harlow.

"Hey, Easy, how about coming to lunch with me and

giving me a quick blowjob?" he remarks. "I'll even buy you lunch."

Her smile fades and anger burns in her eyes. I feel it, the words he spat at her that probably burn and scar her skin.

"Fuck off," we both say at the same time, throwing the douchebag off balance.

He skids to a halt, glancing between the two of us. For a moment, he looks unsure of what to do. But then a shit-eating grin consumes his face.

"Who's your friend?" he asks Harlow while looking at me. "You can bring her, too, and take turns."

Her eyes darken as she turns toward him. "Yeah, there's just one problem with that. In order for either of us to suck you off, we'd have to be able to actually find your tiny penis and, from what I've heard, that could take us all of lunchtime, and I need to eat."

He glares at her. "Screw you, Easy. You think you're so damn special because your daddy's got all this money"—he steps toward her—"but you're nothing but an easy lay who hides behind her big brother."

She curls her fingers into fists. "Maybe I should text my big brother and let him know what's up? I'm sure he's with Zay and Jax, too." She inches toward him. "What do you say? You want me to tattletale on you?"

His glare deepens. "Always taking the easy way out and living up to your name." His glare shifts to a smirk as he steps back and saunters off, but not before grinning at me. "I'll see you around, new girl."

Harlow flips him the middle finger as he walks off and rounds the corner.

"God, I freakin' hate people at this school," she mutters. "But Carter is one of the worst. He's so damn arrogant and his ego is so overinflated."

I want to ask her a lot of things, like what his deal is, why he calls her easy. But having been bullied for most of my life, I can pretty much put two and two together.

Instead, I crack a joke. "He probably has to be that way to overcompensate for his tiny penis."

She chuckles softly, turning to me. "Yeah, probably." She pauses, considering something, tilting her head to the side. "You want to go to lunch with me? My brother is letting me drive his car. I'm going to this diner that has the best fries ever. We might be a little late getting back, but trust me, it'll be totally worth it."

I hesitate, thinking about how I'm supposed to meet Dixie May behind the dumpsters right after lunch is over.

Harlow misinterprets my silence, her smile fading. "Or not. It's totally fine if you don't want to."

"No, it's not that I don't want to. I'm just supposed to meet my cousin and give her her makeup case that she left in the car ..." I stop myself.

What am I doing?

Seriously, what am I doing?

This is the first time in forever that I have a chance to make a friend, and I'm going to toss it away because I need to give Dixie May her makeup case? Screw that! And I'm already in trouble anyway.

"You know what? My cousin can wait until after school," I tell Harlow. "I'd love to go to lunch."

Her smile returns. "Awesome."

Yeah, definitely awesome.

Maybe this day won't turn out as bad as I thought.

Yeah, talk about jinxing myself.

Because literally, three seconds after I have the thought, I receive a text.

Unknown: I know who you are, and I know what you did.

8

RAVEN

GREAT. *Who did Dixie May tell?* is the first thought I have. This text also means she's given out my phone number.

This revelation makes me about twenty times more grateful that I'm going to lunch with Harlow, not only so I can avoid people, but because I'm standing up Dixie May and her makeup case.

Apparently, the message distracts me enough that even Harlow, who barely knows me, can tell something's wrong.

"Is everything okay?" she inquires as we push open the doors and step outside into the sunlight.

I nod and try to force myself to smile. "Yeah, everything's great."

She arches a brow. "You sure about that? You kind of sound ... I don't know, deflated."

"Well, I'm not." I force a cheery tone, but it's completely obvious that it's forced.

God, I suck. It's a good thing I don't work undercover.

She gives a dramatic sigh, walking backward in front of me. "Okay, first rule of us being friends is we can't lie to each other. I loathe liars. It's like a deal breaker for me."

I press my lips together with uncertainty. While I want to tell her about the message, that'll also lead to me telling her about my past. And I can't do that right now. Not when she just implied we could be friends.

"It really is nothing," I say, my boots scuffing against the sidewalk. "I just ..." I blow out an exhale as she stares me down hard. Like really, *really* hard. "Dude, you seriously have the scariest interrogation face ever."

"Oh, I know," she assures me confidentially. "I learned from the best. I also learned how to crack someone open from the best."

"Who's the best?" I ask, curious and also trying to change the subject.

She drags her finger across her lips. "Nope. Not telling until you do."

I hesitate, unsure what to do. Back in the day, before my parents died, I used to have friends. I think I might be out of practice now.

"I got this weird message," I reply vaguely. "But it's not really a bad deal."

A crease forms between her brow. "What'd it say?"

I chew on my bottom lip, deliberating how much I should confess. "If I tell you, you have to promise not to ask questions, so I don't have to lie. Because I can't tell you much about it. Not yet anyway."

She squints against the sunlight as she studies me closely. "Okay, I think I can do that."

A breath eases from my lips as I retrieve my phone from out of my pocket and hand it to her. She takes the phone from me, reads it, then glances up at me with question marks filling her eyes.

"I ..." She smashes her lips together, pausing. "You have no idea who it's from?"

I shrug. "My best bet is my cousin had someone send it to me."

"Your cousin?" she asks. "Wait—is she blonde and kind of a bitch?"

I nod. "Yep. That'd be the one."

"She's the one you were worried about giving the makeup case, too, right?"

I nod again.

"Why do you think it's her? And why did you guys move here at the same time, if you don't mind me asking."

"You're fine." In fact, her questions aren't that awful. Well, unless they lead to certain kinds of follow-up questions. "I think it's her because she threatens to tell people stuff about me all the time. And usually, she does. And we moved here at the same time because I live with her family."

She hesitates. "Where's your family?"

Anxiety clutches my throat. "They ... They died a while ago."

Pity fills her eyes as she slows to a stop near the curb. "I'm sorry." She swallows audibly. "My mom died, too, when I was born, actually, during childbirth."

I stop in front of her, my heart aching for her. "I'm sorry."

She dismisses me with a shrug. "You don't need to say you're sorry. I just wanted to tell you so you'd know that I kind of understand what it feels like to lose someone. Not that I ever knew my mom." She mutters the last part then turns around and starts walking again, across the parking lot.

A few people are here and there, and I catch some of them glancing my way. It makes me cringe. Do they know who I am? Do they know what I did?

I hurry up and walk beside Harlow. "Just because you never knew her, doesn't mean you can't be sad over it. You still lost time with her."

She glances at me with a small smile on her face. "Thanks. I know this is going to sound weird, but I kind of needed to hear that."

"It doesn't sound weird at all." Honestly, it's what I wish someone would've said to me.

Her lips pull up into a half-smile. Then she loops her arms through mine and practically starts skipping. "Yeah, you and I are definitely going to become friends," she declares with great confidence. "And I might have a solution to your little texting problem. Or, at least, a way to figure out who's texting you."

"Really?" I inquire with intrigue.

She nods, strands of her hair falling into her eyes. "Yep. I know people."

"What sort of people?" I wonder as we slow down beside the most gorgeous baby blue Camaro I've ever seen.

My dad was really into classic cars and had a firebird he was fixing up before he died. It was around the same year as this Camaro and looked similar.

Memories start to stir inside me, but I hastily stifle them, not wanting to lose my shit in front of the first potential friend I've had in years.

"People who can find out all sorts of secrets. Even secrets people have worked really hard to bury." She lets out a wicked laugh that echoes across the parking lot.

I can't help laughing, and she grins, fishing her phone from her back pocket.

"Let me just send them a text and see if they're

down." She starts to type a message, but then pauses, glancing up at me. "As long as you're cool with that."

I dither. "Will this person respect my request not to have to answer questions about the text?"

She nods. "If I tell them to, they will."

"How much will they charge me?"

"Nothing, since you're going through me."

I'm still reluctant. "But even if I find out who sent the text, does it really even matter? I mean, it's not like I can make them keep my secret a secret."

A sly smile curls at her lips. "Wanna bet?"

Again, I'm intrigued. "No. Not with that creepy smile you just gave me."

She laughs. "So, you down then?"

Am I? Because truthfully, this is all sort of weird. I mean, who is this girl who knows people who can track numbers and keep people quiet?

Then again, I'm the girl that's responsible for her parents getting killed, so who am I to judge? Plus, if Dixie May is the culprit behind the messages, maybe Harlow can help me get her to shut her mouth.

Yeah, I like the sound of that.

"All right, let's do it," I tell her.

And once again, for the second time today, I'm left crossing my fingers that this decision doesn't come back to bite me in the ass.

9

HUNTER

Picking up the forms for basketball ends up not taking as long as I thought, since the coach ended up having to run home for something. He likes to chitchat a lot so, without his commentary as the team members are filling out forms, it goes by quicker. Like, a hell of a lot quicker.

In fact, if I hurry my ass up, I might be able to grab a bite to eat instead of going to the cafeteria like I'd plan. Of course, since I let Harlow borrow my car, I'll have to walk to someplace close by.

Dammit, I really didn't think this through very well.

Still, walking somewhere is better than eating cafeteria food, even if I have to do it alone since Zay and Jax got in-school suspension for getting caught ditching third period.

"Hunter!" someone shouts behind me as I head for

the exit doors.

When I peer over my shoulder, I spot this girl, Katy, that I hooked up with at a party jogging after me down the hallway.

"Shit," I mutter, quickening my pace. The last thing I need is to waste my lunchtime dealing with drama, something that always comes by talking to Katy.

I hate that I put myself in these situations, and sadly, I kind of have a habit of it. It's why Jax was so harsh with me when he caught me wanting to talk to Ravenlee. I have a knack for hooking up then the girl getting pissed when I don't want to be in a relationship. And I feel bad, but at the same time, I'm way too messed up to be able to be a decent boyfriend. Not to mention even the idea of getting close to anyone scares the hell out of me.

"Hunter!" she shouts again. "I need to talk to you!"

My phone buzzes from inside my pocket, but I ignore it as I burst out the door and quicken my pace to a jog, heading for the sidewalk that lines the front of the school. When I spot my car still parked in the parking lot, I veer right and rush over to it, wondering if Harlow changed her mind about leaving for lunch.

As I near it, though, I see Harlow standing by the trunk with her phone in her hand. And she's not alone. A girl is standing beside her with her back turned toward me —a girl with hair like raven feathers and legs that go on for miles.

Raven.

I hesitate for a fleeting moment, remembering what happened between her and Zay this morning. Not that I blame Raven—Zay can be a dick sometimes—but I also know he'd get pissed at me if he knew I was hanging out with her.

"Hunter!" Katy yells from across the parking lot, causing everyone in the vicinity to look at me, including Harlow and Raven, who appear confused at first, but then Harlow's gaze zeroes in on Katy running after me.

"Oh my God." She busts up laughing.

"Just shut it," I hiss as I reach her. "And get me out of here, please." When she doesn't budge, I grow impatient. "Harlow," I warn.

"Oh, fine." She hurries to the driver's side. "But I'm driving. And you owe me a favor." She gives Raven this weird smile from over the roof, to which Raven looks at her like she's crazy, something that's a pretty common occurrence around Harlow and has made it difficult for her to make friends. So that leaves me wondering how her and Raven ended up together. Not that I'm going to take the time to ask right now. Nope. I just slip my fingers through Raven's and tug her toward the passenger side of the car.

She gapes at me as she stumbles after me. "What're you doing?"

I yank open the door. "Making a quick exit." Then I

slide into the front bench seat and drag her in with me, maybe with a little too much force because she ends up falling on top of me. I don't bother trying to help her sit up; I just yank the door shut and yell at Harlow to, "Drive!"

Laughing her ass off, Harlow revs up the engine and peels out of the parking space, right as Katy reaches the back end of my car. She puts her hands on her hips and glares at us as we speed away.

Deep down, I know this little ditching attempt is only temporary and that she'll find me at school sometime soon and probably be more pissed off than she was to begin with. But what can I say? I like to procrastinate when it comes to this type of stuff.

I let out a breath of relief. "Man, that was close."

Raven sits up, her fingers still tangled with mine. "Did you really have to pull me in so hard?"

"Yeah, sorry about that," I apologize. "I kind of panicked."

"Really?" she mocks. "Because you seemed so collected to me."

Harlow busts up laughing while I crack a small smile. Damn, I forgot how amusing this girl's mouth is. Of course, if she's friends with Harlow, there's definitely no way I can try to hook up with her now. I'm not about to be responsible for ruining the first potential friendship my sister has had in a while. Plus, I'd feel like an asshole if I added more sadness to Raven's beautiful big eyes, and that sort of stuff is my MO.

"Hey, I think I handled being chased by a total lunatic really well," I insist through a bit of laughter.

Raven's brow curves upward. "Why's she a total lunatic?"

I give her a *really?* look. "She just chased me through the school hallway and across the parking lot."

"You didn't have to run from her," she reminds me. "You could've just heard what she had to say."

"I pretty much know what she has to say," I mumble with a sigh.

"How?" she questions. "Because you're a mind reader."

Harlow giggles. "Dude, he probably thinks he is."

I lean forward and elevate my brows. "*I* think that? You literally tried to convince me you were one like an hour ago."

"That's because I am one," she quips with a sassy smile.

Raven laughs at that.

Great. I'm outnumbered.

Maybe I should've taken my chances with Katy.

No, I take that back.

"Why were you running from her anyway?" Raven wonders, reclining back in the seat with her eyes trained on me.

I'll admit, it's a lot to take in—her full attention on me. I know this is going to sound odd, but usually, when people look at me, they're not really looking at me. Or, well, what's underneath my good looks and wealth. Raven, though, she genuinely wants to know the answer to her question, wants to know what's going on with me.

It's hard to take in.

And I really don't want to tell her, because it'll make me sound bad. And I don't want to sound bad to her.

"I already told you—because she's a total lunatic." I give a teasing grin.

Her lips quirk into an adorable half-grin. "Okay, say she is a total lunatic; that still doesn't explain in detail why she was chasing you across a school parking lot."

I don't want to tell her, don't want to explain to her that I hooked up with Katy and that it more than likely has something to do with that.

"He probably hooked up with her," Harlow chimes in. "And now she wants to be boyfriend and girlfriend." She sneers the last part.

I slant forward to glare at Harlow, but she only gives a cheeky grin.

"Thanks for that," I tell her dryly.

"You're welcome," she replies cheerfully. "I don't know why you're trying to keep your manwhore status a secret. Katy already told Raven all about you and your friends."

My gaze drifts to Raven. "You talked to Katy?"

She nods, tucking a strand of hair behind her ear. "It was right before I met Harlow."

"And she told you about me, Zay, and Jax?" I question.

What a brave, stupid girl. Katy, I mean. She should know better than to gossip about me and my friends. If word gets back to Zay, he'll want to retaliate. Not like physically or anything like that. No, Zay likes to plot his revenge way more discreetly, through hacking and destroying people's lives via the internet.

"What all did she tell you?" I ask Raven while stretching my arm across the back of the seat, right behind her.

She lifts a shoulder. "I don't know. She basically just said you guys were scary and that I should stay away from you. She also already told me you two hooked up."

"She really told you that."

"Yep. And she didn't seem that pleased when I said you and I had talked to each other."

The corners of my lips twitch. "You told her you talked to me?"

"Yeah ..." A crease forms between her brow. "What's so weird about that?"

"I don't know ..." I bite back my amusement, telling myself not to say the words that are burning on the tip of my tongue. Apparently, though, I have self-control issues, which I guess really isn't new news. "I was just thinking about how I must've been stuck on your mind."

"Oh my God," Harlow groans, her head bobbing back. "I think I'm gonna puke. Seriously, dude, is that how you get so many girls to swoon over you? Because, if it is, then I've lost all hope for the female population."

Raven smiles at that, and so do I.

"What?" I say innocently. "I was just saying something that's probably pretty true."

"No way," Raven says amusedly. "You weren't stuck on my mind. Katy brought you guys up because she saw what happened between me and Zay in class. Speaking of which"—she rotates in the seat, bringing her leg up so her knee is pressing into the side of my leg, then she rests her elbow on the back of the seat, bringing herself closer to me, I wish on purpose, but I think she's just attempting to get comfortable—"aren't you going to get in trouble for talking to me?"

"With Zay?" I ask, and she nods. I dismiss her with a flick of my wrist. "Nah. I mean, he might not be happy at first, but he'll get over it."

"You sure about that?" she questions, elevating her brow. "Because he seemed pretty pissed off. Plus, your friend Jax kind of told you to stay away from me."

I waver, nibbling on my bottom lip. "That's not what that was about."

"Then what was it about?" she inquires.

I shrug, not wanting to tell her the truth, that Jax was basically warning me not to screw her or I'd probably end up with another Katy situation on my hands. Not that Raven is like Katy. Honestly, if I hadn't been drunk that night, I never would've slept with Katy—she's not my type —but I messed up, like I usually do when I'm drunk. I do it a lot when I'm sober, too.

"You're such screw up," my dad tells me, like he does all the time. "You have all the opportunities in the world, and all you do is piss them away."

He says shit like that all the time. Then he would leave the house, leave her with me. Diane. And while she didn't use to abuse me verbally, she did everything in her power to break me.

I yank myself away from memory lane and breathe in relief as we arrive at the diner.

Thank God. A distraction from my problems.

"So, has Harlow told you anything about this place?" I ask Raven, latching on to the opportunity to change the subject.

She notices, not answering right away, simply staring at me, assessing me. But then she lets it go, her gaze traveling to the old-school diner.

The windows are decorated with neon lights, the waitresses wear roller skates, and to order, you park near the marquee and the waitress brings your food to your car on a tray.

"She said they have the best fries," Raven answers while studying the menu. She gets this weird, almost panicked look on her face and sinks her teeth into her bottom lip.

"They have great milkshakes, too," I tell her, rolling down my window and letting the autumn breeze blow in.

"I think I'm just gonna get fries," she tells me. "I'm not really that hungry."

"No way," Harlow says as she shuts off the engine. "You have to get a milkshake and a burger. The fries taste the best when you eat them with a combo."

Raven shifts uncomfortably while chewing on her thumbnail. "It'd really be a waste of food, because there's no way I'm that hungry right now."

"Oh, fine." Harlow pouts. "But next time we come here, you totally have to try some of everything."

Raven laughs at that. "That's a lot of fucking food."

"Yeah, well, if we put our minds to it, I'm sure we can do it." Harlow grins at her.

Raven grins back. "Okay, next time then."

"Awesome." Harlow assesses the menu then, even though she'll probably order what she always does.

I look at the menu, too, trying to figure out what I want today when, out of the corner of my eye, I catch Raven sticking her hand into her pocket and pulling out some cash. Three dollar bills to be exact. It clicks then why she's being weird about ordering food.

She pockets the money quickly as her phone buzzes. She takes it out, checks the messages, and frowns.

"Bad news?" I wonder.

She startles, then looks up at me and shakes her head. "No ... I don't know."

"Is it them again?" Harlow asks her.

"I ..." Raven hesitantly glances at me then at Harlow.

"Oh, don't worry about Hunter," Harlow says. "He's the person who I was gonna ask for help tracking them down."

Wait ... Did she tell Raven I'm one of the owners of The Raven Three, something that's supposed to remain anonymous?

Goddammit, Harlow.

While Raven isn't looking at me, I glare at Harlow, but she just rolls her eyes.

"Stop looking at me like that. Raven's totally trustworthy."

"How can you be so sure? You've known her for like, what? Thirty minutes?" I snap. Of course, when Raven tenses, I feel like a total douchebag. "Sorry," I tell Raven. "I just ... No one's supposed to know who owns my business. It's ... Well, it's important that I keep it a secret."

"I promise I won't say anything," she tells me, offering me the saddest smile I've ever seen. "Trust me; I get wanting to keep shit a secret. And if you don't want to help me, I totally get that, too."

Jesus, those eyes ... the sadness in them ... it's swallowing me whole right now.

Maybe that's why I say what I say next. Or maybe I'm really just as stupid as my father says I am.

"No, I'll help you," I tell her, and relief washes over her pretty features.

"Awesome," Harlow says then pushes open the door. "I have to use the bathroom. If the waitress comes while I'm gone, order me a chocolate shake with extra cherries, a burger without pickles, and a large order of fries." She climbs out of the car, shuts the door, and then heads inside.

Silence briefly stretches between Raven and me as she stares down at her phone.

"So, I'm guessing from the way you're staring at your phone that you received a text from someone anonymous and want me to track it down," I say, breaking the silence.

Nodding, she glances up at me. "It's from an unknown number."

"Can I see it?" I start to reach for her phone, but she wraps her fingers around it.

"Before I show you, can you promise not to ask me questions about the contents of the message?"

"I never do that with my clients." And usually, I don't care. With her, though ... I'm curious about her. Where she comes from. Who she is.

Why she looks so sad.

"Thanks." Then she takes a deep breath and hands me the phone, showing the message.

Unknown: I know who you are, and I know what you did.

Okay, yeah, I want to ask her questions, yet I know I can't.

So, instead, I say, "I can definitely look into this. How long it'll take, though, all depends on what sort of phone the person sent this from. If they just used a blocking app from their own phone, it'll be easy. If it's a burner phone, it might take a bit." I dig my own phone out of my pocket. "I can tell you right now which one it'll be."

I swipe my finger across the screen, open the scanning app, and then put it close enough to her phone so that I can scan it.

She watches in fascination. "Where did you learn how to do this sort of thing?"

"From people who work for my dad." I set the phones on the dashboard. Then I brace myself for her to ask questions about my dad.

Surprisingly, she doesn't.

"That's kind of cool. I mean, that you know how to do this stuff," she says. "I honestly think it's just my cousin. Well, I think my cousin had someone send it."

I glance at her. "Does your cousin often send you ominous messages?"

She nods. "Yeah ... She has a thing for making my life miserable."

I hesitate, unsure if I should ask, but the need to know overwhelms me. "She's that blonde girl, right? The one who started school today, too."

She nods, eyeing me over. "Her name's Dixie May. Have you met her yet?"

I shake my head. "No. I just saw her in the hallway."

"Hmmm ..." she remarks. "I'm surprised she hasn't introduced herself yet."

My brows furrow. "Why's that?"

"Because you're an FH."

"You said that to me in the office, but I still don't know what it means."

She picks at her fingernail. "It's what Dixie May refers to as a fuckable hottie."

I can't stop a grin from spreading across my face. "You think I'm hot?"

She rolls her eyes. "I'm sure you already know that since you literally just had a girl chasing after you."

My grin broadens. "I'm not asking if Katy thinks I'm hot—I already know she does. I was asking if *you* think I'm hot."

Her cheeks turn pink. She's blushing. Actually fucking blushing. And it's by far the cutest thing I've ever seen.

"You're blushing," I tease.

She glares at me, but she's struggling not to smile. "Shut up. I am not."

"You are," I insist. "It's okay, though. It's cute."

She rolls her eyes again. "No, it's not."

"Yeah, it is. It's cute—you're cute." Then I reach up and brush my hand across her cheek. I'm not even sure why I do it, other than maybe I want to see if her skin is as soft as it looks. And it is, if not softer.

A shaky breath fumbles from her lips, her cheeks tinting pink even more. "I'm not cute," she breathes out.

"No. You completely fucking are." I graze my knuckles across her cheek again.

When her eyelashes flutter, I almost kiss her, which I know would be a dumbass move, seeing as how she just befriended my loner sister, and I have a knack for only hooking up. Although, with how easily Raven blushed, I wonder if she's not the hooking up type.

Thankfully, the waitress skates up before I can do something stupid.

I know her from school. Her name is Stella, and she's a year older than me, having graduated last summer. She never went to college, which is kind of a typical thing for this town.

"Hey, Hunter," she greets me with a smile as she skates up to my rolled-down window. "What're you doing sitting in the passenger seat of your own car."

"Harlow wanted to drive," I reply, resting my arm on

the windowsill.

"Right. She's sixteen now," she says as she digs her ordering pad and pen from out of the apron tied around her waist. "That's crazy. I can still remember when she was little and used to color on everything." She laughs softly. "Remember that one time in grade school when she colored all over the school walls."

"I remember." I try to keep my tone light, but the memory was so much darker than Stella realizes. When Harlow and I got home that day from school, the teacher had already informed my dad about what happened. He was livid and started screaming at Harlow to the point where I thought he was going to hit her, so I stepped and lied, saying I was the one who did it, and the teacher was just confused. He struck me so hard my ears rang. It wasn't the first or last time he hit me. "Should've known back then that she'd get into art."

"She's into art?" Stella asks, poising the pen. "I guess I'm not surprised, considering who her big brother is." She smiles at me.

It's a flirty smile, and normally, I'd probably flirt back, but considering I was just flirting with Raven, I keep a friendly tone and smile.

"Yeah, I guess so," I say, scratching my wrist.

"You're an artist?" Raven asks, seeming a bit surprised.

I glance at her with an amused smile on my face. "Sort

of. Why do you sound so surprised?"

She gives a half-shrug. "I just thought you were a jock."

"Jocks can be artists, too," I tell her. "How do you know I'm a jock? Or did Katy tell you?"

"No, I overheard the teacher talking to you about a game or something," she explains. "I was kind of surprised you play sports. You don't really look like the type."

Now I'm beyond amused. "What do I look like I'd be into then?"

Her gaze scrolls up and down me, and then she shrugs. "Well, if I had to stereotype you, I'd say music or art."

"I actually am into both," I inform her. When she gives me a disbelieving look, I wink at her. "I'm a man of many talents."

She shakes her head but smiles, her lips parting.

"Um, I kind of need to take your order," Stella interrupts.

Shit. I'd almost forgotten she was there.

I turn toward her. "Right. Sorry about that."

"It's no problem." She offers me a friendly, not flirty smile. "What can I get you?"

I order what Harlow told me, then order my own food, but double it so Raven can eat more than just some fries if she wants.

"Sounds good," Stella says as she jots the order down.

Then she looks at Raven. "And for you?"

"I'll just have fries," Raven says, fiddling with a leather band covering her wrist.

"Really?" Stella questions, eyeing her over. "Wait—you're new here, right?"

She nods. "I just moved here this weekend."

She smiles. "Well, welcome to our town."

"Thanks," Raven replies, giving her a small smile.

Stella smiles one last time at her then looks at me. "I'll go put in your order. It'll probably be ready in about fifteen minutes." Then she skates off to the order window.

"So you're really an artist, musician, and a jock?" Raven asks, going right back to the conversation.

I turn to her and nod. "I'm not really into the same kind of art as Harlow, though. She likes to sketch and paint while I'm into photography. As for the musician stuff, I'm not in a band or anything. I just like to play the guitar sometimes. And as for the jock thing, I play basketball."

"That's a lot of stuff," she comments, combing her fingers through her hair. "I don't even have one talent, let alone three."

"Everyone has a talent. So, either you haven't found yours yet, or you just don't want to tell me."

"If that's true, then it's definitely the first," she says. "It's awesome you can play the guitar. And the photography thing is interesting."

"Not impressed by the basketball thing, huh?" I tease.

She dithers. "It's not that I'm not impressed. I've just had bad experiences with jocks."

"Not all of them are bad," I assure her. "I'm not. I promise."

"You don't seem bad, and I don't really think all of them are bad. It's just ..." She sighs. "I guess I've just had a lot of bad experiences with jocks, but that might partly be because of Dixie May ..." She shrugs again, then offers me a cute, little smile. "I'll try not to stereotype you into that group."

I smile at her, but I'm a bit unsettled with what she's saying. She keeps bringing up her cousin, which makes me want to know ... "You said you live with your cousin?"

She gives a reluctant nod. "Unfortunately."

"Does she live with your family? Or do you live with hers?"

As her gaze drops to her lap, I have my answer. And I feel bad for even bringing it up.

"I live with hers ... My parents died a handful of years ago, so ..." She sucks in a breath and looks up at me. "Yeah, anyway, Dixie May and I have never gotten along, which you've probably caught on to."

I nod and proceed with caution. "Has she always been mean to you?"

She nods. "But honestly, up until I had to move in with them, I barely knew her." She gives a short pause.

"To be honest, in a way, I kind of feel bad for her. Her mom—my aunt—is a real piece of work, and Dixie May is basically her doppelganger."

"So, she's been taught bitchery."

She smiles at that. "Yeah, I guess you could say that."

"Thankfully, it didn't wear on you." At least, she doesn't seem that way so far. And she's been nice to Harlow.

"You sure about that?" she questions. "I think you're forgetting what happened between me and Zay."

"Nah. Zay was an asshole. You were just defending yourself."

"I could've just changed seats."

"And Zay could've just left you alone. The seats aren't assigned anyway." If Zay heard me right now, he'd lose his shit. But what I'm saying is true. Zay didn't need to be such a dick to Raven. Granted, he's a dick to almost everyone. "You shouldn't take it personally," I add. "Zay's kind of a dick to everyone."

"So, it's not just me?"

"Nah. If anyone had sat in his seat, he would've reacted the same way. Although, anyone who knows him would've never sat in his seat."

"Hmm ..." She rubs her lips together, and again, I find myself wanting to kiss her. "So, what you're saying is that tomorrow I should sit in a different seat."

I start to nod then hesitate. "Well, that all depends."

Her brows furrow. "On what?"

"On if you can find a seat available by me."

"You wanna sit by me?" she asks, sounding shocked.

"Sure. I mean, we can be friends, right?" *Just friends*, I have to remind myself. Because, if she's going to be friends with Harlow, too, I can't ruin that by … well, being myself. Harlow hasn't had any good friends for a long time, and she's the most important person in my life.

"Friends." She says the word funnily.

"What's so funny about that?" I wonder amusedly.

She gives a shrug. "I just haven't had a lot of those in my life. And now, suddenly, I have two people offering to be my friend … It's a little weird."

The way she says it, as if it's so surprising that someone would want to be her friend, makes my chest tightens a bit. I've been lucky in my life to have two best friends since I was in grade school. I've seen Harlow struggle to make friends though, so I've seen how hard it is to go through life friendless.

"Well, welcome to the land of weird, then," I tell her with a grin.

She traces her lips with the tip of her tongue, appearing amused by something. "You say that like I already accepted your offer of friendship," she teases.

My grin widens, but then I jut out my bottom lip. "So, you're saying you don't wanna be my friend? Way to break my heart."

She bites back a smile. "Fine. I'll be your friend. Just stop pouting."

I only pout more, and she playfully pinches my side.

I laugh, gripping my side. "So vicious." I lower my hand then, grinning, I pinch her back on the side.

Instead of laughing, she winces, her face contorting with pain.

I jerk back. "What's wrong?"

"It's nothing," she mumbles shakily.

It's clearly not nothing, and I'm about to attempt to get the truth out of her, but Harlow returns to the car.

"Please tell me the waitress took our order already," she says as she climbs into the driver's seat and shuts the door.

"She did," Raven tells her, wiping her expression clean of all signs that she was in pain. But just because she erased the look, doesn't mean I'm going to forget it. No, the look is branded in my mind.

I want to know what caused it. Want to know all about the girl with hair like raven feathers and eyes so hauntingly beautiful. The girl I just told I want to be her friend.

Just her friend.

Just friends.

The thing is ...

That might be a lie.

Shit, I'm so screwed.

10

RAVEN

EVERYTHING WAS GOING great until he pinched my side. Then it all came rushing back to me, every horrible moment, every scar. Everything he's done to me. But I do my best to play it off, hoping to God that he doesn't ask questions. Luckily, Harlow shows up and offers a fantastic distraction.

"That was the longest piss ever," Hunter remarks after his sister has climbed back in. His brow arches upward in accusation, perplexing the hell out of me.

Harlow adjusts the rearview mirror and examines her expression. "What can I say? I drank a thirty-two ounce soda for breakfast."

Hunter just shakes his head while thrumming his fingers against his knee, clearly annoyed.

And me? I'm totally confused and feeling really

uncomfortable. Before the awkwardness gets too out of hand, though, the waitress skates up with our order. She smiles as she balances the tray on Hunter's half-rolled down window.

"Just honk if you need anything, okay?" She smiles at him before skating back toward the order window.

"*Just honk if you need anything,*" Harlow mocks while twirling a strand of hair around her finger. "And I mean, *anything* at all."

Hunter picks up a burger. "She didn't say anything at all." He hands Harlow the burger.

"Yeah, so? She meant it." Harlow unwraps the burger then glances at me. "Something you should know about this little town that you now live in—almost every girl around your age, give or take a couple of years, is freakin' obsessed with my brother."

"Not every girl," Hunter protests, handing me some fries.

I breathe in the salty goodness. "I don't know. From what I've seen so far, it seems like you've got a ton of admirers."

Hunter gives me an unimpressed stare but is struggling not to smile. "You say admirers. I say stalkers."

Harlow snorts a laugh. "Like you don't encourage them."

"I *don't* encourage them," he insists, collecting

another burger. "They just ... I don't know ... I don't know why they're so obsessed with me."

Did he seriously just almost quote *Mean Girls?*

"Dude, you so did not just say that," Harlow and I say at the same time. Then we both yell out, "Jinx!" It's a real bonding moment, let me tell you.

Hunter's gaze shifts between us, a trace of a confused smile playing at his lips. "Okay, I'm so confused. What're you two screaming about?"

"*Mean Girls,*" we both say then laugh.

His confusion only magnifies. "What?"

"It's a movie," I explain. "A total chick flick. You should watch it."

"You think I'm the type of guy to watch a chick flick?"

"Actually, yeah, maybe." I say it mostly to mess with him, but he does sort of seem like the type of guy who would. "You should watch it."

He chuckles, rolling his tongue in his mouth. "I'll tell you what; I'll watch it, but only if you watch it with me."

"Hey." Harlow points a finger at Hunter. "No way. You are so not trying to steal my new best friend."

"I'm not trying to steal her," he assures her while smiling at me. "Raven and I are friends, though. We already decided this while you were taking the world's freakin' longest piss."

"Maybe I have a UTI?" Harlow quips then takes a huge bite of her burger.

"TMI, little sis," Hunter gripes. "And FYI, if you do, it's probably from all the fucking soda you're drinking in the morning." He moves to hand me the burger.

I shake my head. "I just got fries, remember?"

"I know. And I know you said you weren't that hungry, but I can't let you do this the wrong way," he explains. "The first time you eat here, you have to go all-out so you can get the full experience."

"I ..." Shit. I don't have enough money to cover a full meal. I can barely afford to pay for the fries without chipping in for a tip. "I ... I didn't bring enough money with me." What I don't say is that I'll never bring enough money with me.

I get three bucks a day for lunch from the money that my aunt and uncle give me from an allowance that was left for them after my parents passed away. It's to be used to feed and clothe me. There's hardly money, though, something my aunt and uncle like to remind me of a lot.

"It's okay. I got you covered," Hunter says then winks at me.

My discomfort grows. I really don't like it when people try to pay for things for me. "It really is fine if I just eat fries."

"Let him pay for it," Harlow chimes in. "I'll chip in half, too, so it's just not totally from my brother." When I start to protest, Harlow adds, "I've never gotten to buy a best friend her lunch before, so if you decline, you're totally taking this new experience away from me." She gives me an evil grin.

While I'm perfectly aware she's not being completely serious, I decide to stop arguing and accept the offer. But I make a vow to figure out a way to treat them to lunch sometime and pay them back.

"Fine," I agree.

Hunter smiles as he hands me the burger. Then he extends his fist toward his sister for a fist bump. "You and I make a pretty good team, little sis."

She taps her knuckles against his then takes a huge bite of her burger. "For sure. We should make a business of it, and our slogan can be, 'how to bully your new best friend into eating lunch.' "

I shake my head but can't help laughing. Of course, then I take a bite of my burger, and that laugh turns into a moan as I nearly have a foodgasm.

"Holy crap, that's good." I lick a droplet of fry sauce off my bottom lip and notice Hunter staring at me with a weird look on his face. "What?" I ask. "Do I have sauce on my face or something?"

He shakes his head. "You're good." He stares at me for a beat longer then tears his attention off me, focusing on our phones as one of them releases a series of beeps. He scoops up his phone, looks at the screen, and then a crease forms between his brow. "That's weird."

Worry stirs through me. "What is it?"

His gaze lifts to mine. "It wouldn't track the exact location of the phone, but it did give me an estimate."

"Is that not normal?" I ask as I pop a fry into my mouth.

"Not usually. But it's not completely abnormal," he tells me. "What's weird, though, is that it says the location is in Wyoming."

"Is that where you're originally from?" Harlow wonders.

A knot forms in my stomach. "I ... I was born in a town there and lived there for a while." I lived there until I had to move in with my aunt and uncle, right after I killed my parents.

RAVEN

HERE's the thing about what happened to my parents. While there's no proof that I actually killed them, there's also no proof that I didn't. And the only fact I can go on are little images that I vaguely remember. But most of that day and a few days before and after are nothing but a blur of emptiness. The theory is that the trauma made me forget what happened, which would be believable, except the few memories that I can recall contain images of blood staining my hands, of being near my parents' bodies, of me holding a knife. The latter, though, no one else knows about because I've kept it a secret. And for a good reason, since some believe I killed my parents. In fact, I was taken to the police station when it happened and questioned multiple times, but they couldn't find any hardcore proof, so they released me.

When my aunt and uncle found out that I was under suspicion, they ate that shit up. And so did Dixie May. What I don't get is why they hated me so much before they discovered I might have done it. Even the few times I'd met them before my parents died, they despised me.

"So you can't tell who sent the text then?" I double-check, trying to steer the conversation away from Wyoming and everything that happened there.

"Not yet," Hunter says. "Give me a few days, and I'll probably be able to find out."

I could tell him not to worry about it, but now that I know it's sent from someone in Wyoming, that eliminates the sender being Dixie May, which leaves me wondering who it is.

"Okay. Thanks." I collect my phone from the dash and pocket it.

"While I work on it, I'll have to have your phone," Hunter informs me as he collects a milkshake from the tray and hands it to me. "So we'll have to get together, probably after school. Tryouts are starting tomorrow, so it'll have to be after that."

"It's fine if you can't," I tell him then take a sip of the delicious milkshake. He's so busy, and I'm making it worse.

He carries my gaze. "I can. We'll just have to do it a bit later. Maybe we can meet up for dinner or something."

"It sounds like a date," Harlow remarks, dabbing her face with a napkin.

"It's not a date," Hunter assures me then throws Harlow a dirty look. "If you don't knock it off, I'm gonna drink your entire shake."

She narrows her eyes. "You wouldn't dare."

"Try me," he challenges with a cock of his brow.

Harlow glares at him but keeps her lips sealed. Hunter smirks at her then hands her the shake before returning his attention to me.

"Let's exchange numbers so I can get ahold of you," he says casually, as if it's not a big deal.

But it is a huge deal, at least to me. I've never exchanged numbers with anyone before, never had any friends until now.

Maybe this move isn't as bad as I thought it was going to be.

I just need to make sure my past stays a secret, or else I'll lose these friendships before they even start.

12

RAVEN

After we finish eating, we head back to school. We're a bit late, and normally, I'd be bothered by this and have to take a few hits before I walk into class, but I'm riding a friendship high right now, so I decide not to.

"What class do you have next?" Hunter asks me as the three of us wander toward the entrance of the school.

Since the bell has already rang, hardly anyone is around, except for us and a few others.

"Bio, I think." I dig out my schedule that I tucked inside my pocket and check. "Yep, bio."

"With Ms. Mellie?" he asks, stuffing his hands into his pockets.

I nod as we reach the door. "Yep."

"Cool. I'm heading close to there. I'll walk you." He

opens the door for me and lets me walk in. He also waits for Harlow to enter before he walks in himself.

Harlow lets out a snort. "Wow, this gentleman side of you is new."

"Don't get used to it," he jokes. "I'm just trying to impress my new friend." He winks at me.

A smile tugs at my lips, but I try not to let it get too huge, not wanting to seem like a total weirdo.

"Speaking of new friends." Harlow faces me while retrieving her phone from her pocket. "Let's swap digits."

"Good idea." I attempt to appear as collected as possible as we trade numbers and enter them into our phones, but this is the second time I've done this today—and in my entire life—so I'm a little jacked up. Hopefully, they don't notice.

Once we're done, she waves bye as she starts off in the opposite direction we're heading in, calling out, "I'll text you tonight."

I wave back then Hunter and I head off in the other direction.

"I'm glad you're going to be friends with my sister," he says as we slowly make our way to our classes. "She doesn't have a lot of friends, and you seem like you're just the right amount of weird to get along with her well." He nudges me lightly in the side while smiling at me.

"You think I'm weird?" I question, already knowing I am.

"From what I can tell, you are a little bit. Don't worry; that's a compliment."

"I wasn't worried," I assure him. "You don't seem that normal either, FYI."

"Oh, I'm not," he tells me. "I'm completely and one-hundred percent weirdo."

I giggle at that.

A huge smile takes over his face as he slows to a stop in front of a closed classroom door. "This is your class," he tells me. "If you don't want to be marked tardy, just tell Ms. Mellie that you couldn't find the classroom because you're new. She's nice enough that she'll let it slide."

"Okay, thanks. I will." I move to step inside the classroom, but he captures my arm and stops me.

"I wanted to also say that Zay ..." He dithers for a moment. "I'm going to talk to him. Everything will be cool by tomorrow, okay?"

"You don't have to do that. He's your friend."

"It's not a big deal," he vows, letting go of my arm and backing away. "I'll text you tonight so we can set up a time to do that phone thing."

I nod, watching him walk away, feeling a bit ... I don't know, happy maybe? It's been a long time since I've felt this way, but I'm pretty sure that's what this floating feeling is.

Of course, right before I walk into the classroom, I receive a text that makes that cloud go *poof*.

Bitchy Bitch of the West: Thanks for standing me up after lunch. You're going to regret this big time.

13

HUNTER

I END up having to meet Diane by myself since Jax and Zay are still stuck in in-school suspension. To say I'm not thrilled would be the understatement of the year. But at least the diner is relatively busy. That means I can get in and out super-fast, and Diane can't stop me. Not without causing a scene. And if she did and word got back to my father ...

Yeah, she's not going to cause a scene.

I order a drink and a piece of pie before finding a booth in the far back corner. I've already messaged Diane that I'm here, and she replied that she'd be here in just a few.

I'm sitting there, bored out of my mind, when I decide to text Raven to distract myself. Not that I think she'll reply since she's in class.

Me: How's my favorite new friend?

Weirdly, she responds within seconds.

Raven: I'm not doing great at all.

Me: What's wrong?

Raven: Well, when I signed up for classes, everything was full except for beginners art. So here I am, sitting at a table with a pencil and am supposed to be trying to draw a vase, but mine looks like a taco.

I'm mid-drink as I read this, so soda sprays all over the table when I laugh. I grab a couple of napkins, wipe up the mess, and reply back.

Me: I seriously just spit my soda out all over the table. How in the heck can you make a vase look like a taco?

Raven: By having zero art skills. You know that saying: I have two left feet. Well, I think I have two left hands or something.

I smile.

Me: Well, it's a good thing you have two friends who are awesome artists.

Raven: Yeah, but you can't really teach art, can you? You're just kind of born with that skill.

Me: That might be partly true, but we can

help you improve, at least enough that your vase won't look like a taco anymore.

Raven: Thank God, because I seriously spent the last fifteen minutes convincing myself that it won't be that bad if I fail out of art.

Me: You won't fail. I promise. Harlow and I've got your back.

It takes her a moment to respond.

Raven: Thanks. I appreciate everything you guys have done for me. It's been nice not to have to go through my first day of school completely friendless.

She's said a couple of things that have made me question if she had friends before. And this message only makes me wonder that more. How, though? How can such a beautiful, amusing girl not have any friends?

I'm about to reassure her that she won't be friendless anymore when a shadow falls over the table. I stiffen as a folder is tossed onto the table in front of me.

Sucking in a breath, I glance up at Diane.

She's smiling, not in a friendly way, though; more like how a monster smiles at their prey.

"That's the file on the new sheriff," she states, strangely not taking a seat. "It's the info your father has managed to collect on him so far. There's not much and even less information about his family." She places a hand on top of the folder, leaning down toward me. "You're to find out as much as you can about everyone he's close to then report back to me, understand?"

"Yep." I manage to keep an even tone as I grab the folder and yank it out from underneath her hand, causing her to stumble a little.

Glaring at me, she smooths her hands over her hair. "Careful how you treat me." She leans in, lowering her voice. "I'm the one who tells your father whether or not you're doing a good job ..." She traces her finger along my cheek and whispers, "I can either make you look terrific or make it look like you don't respect him, that you're the epitome of your mother."

I jerk back, shock whipping through me. "What?"

She gives me a cruel smile. "What? Did I say something that confused you?"

"You ..." I swallow hard, balling my hands into fists. "Why did you bring up my mother? And why did you make it sound like ...?" Like my father did something to her.

"Did I?" she questions, tapping her finger against her lips. "I don't remember doing so."

I want to wring her neck, not just for now, but for everything she's done to me. But if I do, she'll tell my father and I'll be punished. That doesn't mean I'm going to let this go.

She knows something about my mom, and I'm going to find out what.

Grinning at me one last time, she turns to leave. "Text me tonight with an update," she calls out over her shoulder. "Or I'll pay you a visit at your house tonight." She strolls away, past the booths, and exits the diner.

I release a shaky breath, fighting back every instinct I have to chase after her and drag the truth from her stupid lips. If I'm going to get the truth out of her, I need to come up with a plan. But first, I need to look into this, because the last thing I need is to have her showing up at my house tonight.

I open the file and start sifting through the few papers inside it. The waitress shows up eventually with my slice of pie and a drink. Whoever was looking into the town sheriff before me either didn't do a good job or the sheriff has done a fantastic job at keeping information on him a secret. There's hardly anything in here. Just some details about his position at his old job, where he moved from— basic stuff like that. But something does capture my attention. A few names on the paper or one in particular.

Ravenlee Wilowwynter.

The sheriff is her uncle. Why did I not put this together before?

Maybe because I was so caught up in the beautiful new girl with the saddest eyes I've ever seen. And as I continue to sort through the papers, I soon discover why. Or at least one of the reasons.

Raven's parents were murdered. That's why she's living with her aunt and uncle.

When I can't find any of the details of what happened, I find a note implying that the police briefly thought Raven had something to do with it. Not that I believe it. The police get stuff wrong all the time. Still, I turn to searching the internet on my phone for more information. But nothing shows up. It's almost like someone has wiped the information clean.

My thoughts drift back to that message Raven had me look into. Was that what this was about? Is she hiding her true identity or something? With how little information is in this folder, I'm wondering if the new sheriff and his family are, too.

"So, Diane's already been here?" Zay suddenly appears and slides in the booth across from me.

Jax is right behind him, taking a seat beside Zay.

"Yeah." My brows pull together. "What the hell are you two doing here? I thought you had in-school suspension."

"We did, but then Jax hacked into Mr. Moleny's computer and found out some interesting search history that could be incriminating if anyone found out," Zay says, grabbing the plate with my half-eaten slice of pie on it.

"So you two blackmailed him into getting out of suspension?" I ask, though it's not really a question, since I pretty much already know the answer.

Jax nods, reclining back into the booth. "We also blackmailed him into giving us a ride here and informed him that if we ever got in-school suspension again, we'd send everyone on the teacher faculty a list of the information."

"*We?*" Zay questions, cocking his brow at Jax.

"Okay, Zay informed him," Jax corrects with an eye roll. "I hacked into the system."

I'm not surprised. Out of the two of them, Zay is way more vocal and daring. Jax has always been the quieter one, while I'm the jokester. Together, we kind of balance each other out, which is why I think we've managed to remain best friends for so long, despite how different we are.

We do have similarities, though, like our messed-up, broken families, corrupt fathers, and painful childhoods. But we rarely speak about that kind of stuff.

"It was a damn good idea. I'm glad, too, because this flying solo thing was getting really old." I slant back and cross my arms, my thoughts wandering back to Ravenlee and how I spent lunch with her.

Okay, maybe my solo time wasn't completely awful. And after reading this file, I want to know more about her.

"What's that look for?" Zay asks as he stuffs a bite of

pie into his mouth.

I lift a shoulder. "I'm just thinking about what's in this file. Or, more like what's *not* in it."

Jax leans forward and rests his arms on the table. "What do you mean?"

"I mean, there's hardly any background info on the town sheriff or his family." I briefly pause. "Or his niece."

"Who's his niece? And what does she have to with this?" Zay asks as he wolfs down another bite of pie.

After what happened between Zay and Raven, I'm hesitant to tell him. But I'll eventually have to since him and Jax will be helping me dig up information on the sheriff.

"You know the new girl?" I ask cautiously.

"The blonde one?" Zay asks. "Or the other fucking one with a death wish?"

"Speaking of which," Jax chimes in, "are those two sisters? Because they don't look or act like it, yet they started school the same day ... I'm a little confused."

"They're cousins," I explain. "The blonde one is Dixie May and is the sheriff's daughter. Raven, the one who got Zay's panties all up in a bunch, is his niece. He got guardianship over her after her parents were murdered."

"She didn't get my panties in a bunch," Zay grumbles, blasting me with a hard look. "She just pissed me off, and for a good reason."

"Sitting in your seat isn't a good reason to get pissed

off at someone," I say. "And besides, she's new."

"I don't give a shit if she's new." Zay stuffs another piece of pie into his mouth. "She should've moved when I told her to."

"Or you could've just asked," Jax tells him quietly.

Zay glares at him, and Jax sighs and mutters, "Or not."

I press my lips together, deciding how much I want to tell them. "I ate lunch with her today. Well, her and Harlow."

Zay drops his fork. "What?"

I shrug then give them a quick recap of how I ended up in my car with Raven and Harlow.

"So you spent like half an hour with Harlow and this new girl," Zay says after I finish, sarcasm oozing from his tone. "I bet that was fun."

"It actually wasn't that bad. I mean, Harlow was kind of a pain in the ass, but not completely. And as for Raven ..." I sink back against the seat, wavering. "Zay, I think you should give her another chance. After talking with her, I think she was just nervous during class. And from what I gathered, I don't think she has a lot of friends."

"So?" Zay mumbles. "How the fuck is that my problem?"

"It's not. But we all know what it's like to be bullied. Not by people at school, but by our families. Plus ..." I pause, treading with caution, "her parents were murdered, Zay. And you of all people should know how badly having to deal with something like that can mess with someone's mind."

Not that Zay's parents were murdered. His older brother was a handful of years ago. The case was never solved, but I think, deep down, all of us know our fathers had something to do with it, since Zay's brother was working for them at the time. Sometimes, when we have free time, we try to look into it ourselves, but we haven't really gotten anywhere so far.

Zay grows quiet then and begins picking at the pie.

"I'm sorry for bringing it up," I tell him apologetically. "I just … I feel bad for her, and I kind of want to try to be her friend, which means you guys have to, too, since we're sort of a package deal." When he says nothing, I add, "If it helps, she felt bad for riling you up during class."

"Did she?" he mumbles, continuing to pick the pie apart.

Sighing, I glance at Jax, hoping he'll help me out.

But all he does is frown. "I don't mean to be an asshole, but do you think you can be just friends with a girl? Especially one who …" He wavers. "Well, one who looks like her."

"What do you mean by 'looks like her'?" I play dumb, knowing exactly what he's referring to.

And he gives me a look that says exactly that. "You know what I'm talking about," he tells me. "She's … Well, she's … good looking—"

Zay snorts a laugh and mumbles something under his breath incoherently.

I roll my eyes and shake my head. "What? You disagree with him or something?"

He looks at me, or more like stares me down hard. "No. I just thought it was funny he used the term good looking."

"Do you have a better word?" I ask.

Zay rolls his eyes as he slumps back in the seat. "We all know she's fucking gorgeous, so we might as well not tiptoe around it." He considers something. "However, whether she's hot or not is beside the point ... Being friends with an outsider is complicated. I mean, for starters, we'd have to keep our jobs a secret, which would be a pain in the ass since our jobs are a huge part of our lives." I must pull a funny face, because Zay's gaze turns accusatory. "Please tell me you didn't already tell her about our jobs."

Jax straightens, worry flooding his features. "Hunter, please say you didn't."

"Okay, I didn't." But it's pretty clear I'm lying, and they both scowl at me. "Look, I didn't tell her everything. She just got a weird text from an unknown number, and I tried to track it down for her."

"Tried?" Zay asks.

"I could only get a vague location," I explain. "But I'm going to continue looking into it for her."

They both look annoyed as hell, and I guess that's kind of understandable.

"Look, if we become friends with her, we can make sure she keeps quiet about it," I say. "Plus, maybe she can help us learn more about her uncle."

"And why do you think she'd help us with that?" Zay says with an arch of her brow. "Her uncle's her family. We're not."

"Yeah, but I got the impression she's not a huge fan of her aunt, uncle, or cousin." I pick up my drink and take a sip, waiting for them to say something. They don't. Finally, I set the glass down and ask, "So, what do you guys think?"

Jax shrugs while fiddling with a straw wrapper. "I'm not opposed to it, but I also don't think we should tell her all our secrets either ... If she told the wrong person the wrong thing ... we could be screwed."

"I know that," I assure him. "We can be cautious around her."

Jax deliberates momentarily then gives a small nod. "Okay, I'm fine with it, I guess."

My gaze skates to Zay, and I lift a brow. "What do you think?"

"I think she's going to drive me crazy," he mutters. "But whatever. If you guys want to be friends with her, I can't stop you."

While that's not a yes, it's probably as close as I'm going to get to one.

"Awesome." Noting the time, I close the file and slide it toward them. "I have to head to tryouts. Go ahead and look through that. There's not much, but it's a start." I stand up, preparing to leave, but then I pause. "Wait—you guys are going to have to ride back with me, since I have the car."

They're already sifting through the papers in the folder, and Zay gives a dismissive shake of his head. "We'll just hang out here for a while and get something to eat. We might go hang out at the bridge and smoke a bowl or two, if we're feeling ambitious," Zay tells me. "Just text us when tryouts are over, and we'll let you know where we're at."

"Okay. Cool." I start toward the door.

"Hunter?" Jax calls out.

I turn around. "Yeah?"

"Good luck," he tells me with a small smile.

"Thanks." I leave the diner feeling pretty good. But as soon as I climb into my car, my thoughts drift right back to Raven.

Who is this beautiful, mysterious girl with sad and familiar eyes?

I hope I can find out.

I also hope I'm not making a mistake by trusting my gut instinct and befriending her.

14

RAVEN

I keep expecting something to happen during school, like show up at my locker and find the word: *murderer* painted across it, which wouldn't be the first time. By the end of the day, however, nothing has happened. So weird. Usually, Dixie May follows through with her threats right away.

I don't relax as I grab my stuff and head out of the school, weaving around people cramming up the hallway. No one glances in my direction. Well, a few people do, but mostly out of curiosity over the new girl. It's a weird feeling, not having people look at me like I'm a freak. But I know it won't last.

Sighing at that thought, I push through the doors and search the area for my aunt's car. Yeah, I know she said she wouldn't give me a ride home, but if I sneak into the car and refuse to get out, she won't have a choice.

But I can't find it anywhere.

So weird. I mean, she has to pick up Dixie May, right? What if Dixie May got a ride home from one of her new friends that I'm sure she's made? Crap, if that's the case, then I'm screwed since I don't even know what bus I'm supposed to be riding.

Sighing, I make a U-turn to go back to the main office and find out. But when I arrive there, no one is at the front desk. I wait a while before the secretary shows up.

"So, how was your first day?" she asks as she plops down in the seat behind the desk.

"Good," I tell her honestly, which is a little weird.

"Good. That's always good to hear." She gives a short pause. "Is there something I can help you with?"

I nod. "I was wondering if you can help me figure out my bus number?"

"Sure." She turns toward the computer. "What's your address?"

When I tell her, she types it in the system then gives me the number.

"I hope you don't need to ride it today, though," she says, rotating the chair back in my direction then glancing at the clock. "The buses have probably already left."

My expression briefly plummets. "Oh."

She offers me a look of pity. "Is there someone you can call for a ride?"

No. But not wanting her to continue to look at me with pity, I nod. "Yeah, I can call my aunt." As tears burn in my eyes, I hurriedly turn to leave. "Thanks for looking that up for me."

"You're welcome," she says as I push out the door and step into the now mostly vacant hallway.

Shit. What am I going to do? I have no damn idea.

So much for a great first day.

Resisting the urge to cry, I wander down the hallway. I could text my aunt and beg her to come get me, but that might not even work. I do a map search and see that the walk home is about seven miles. If I jogged, I could get home in a couple of hours, right before it gets dark.

Seeing no other option, I make my way toward the exit doors then pause as I'm walking by the gym. The doors are shut but have windows, and I can hear the sounds of balls being bounced. When I peek in, I see guys playing basketball. Or, more specifically, Hunter playing basketball. He's only wearing shorts so his chest is on full display. He has a couple of small tattoos, but I'm too far away to tell what they are. He's also lean, defined, and is dripping with sweat. It's ... Well, it's a nice view.

"What're you doing?"

I startle, thinking maybe this is it—the way Dixie May is going to get me back—but then I glance to the side and see Katy standing beside me. I relax just a drop, but not completely, recalling how she chased Hunter across the parking lot.

"I was just watching the tryouts," I say. "Well, glancing at them."

Her gaze flicks from the window to me then she crosses her arms. "Hunter's in there."

"Um, yeah, I know." I adjust the handle of my backpack. "I wasn't watching him, though." Liar. I was totally watching him.

Her brow meticulously arches. "Bullshit. I saw you drive off today with Hunter in his car."

"Well, I was technically with Harlow, Hunter's sister—"

"I know who Hunter's sister is," she cuts me off, stepping toward me. "Everyone does. Everyone also knows she's a freak. So if you're hanging out with her, that makes you a freak. At least, by a technicality."

So over this conversation, I lift my brows. "Okay, I'm gonna go." I move to step around her, but she grabs ahold of my arm.

"Stay away from Hunter," she warns, gripping my arm tightly.

I roughly jerk away from her then lean in. "Don't ever fucking touch me again."

She glares at me, and I glare right back before walking off.

Dude, Hunter was right. She is a crazy lunatic. I'm just glad I decided to go to lunch with Harlow today and not sit down in the cafeteria with her friends.

Once I leave crazy pants behind, I leave the school and embark on the lovely journey home. Okay, lovely might be a stretch. Well, the scenery isn't bad, shifting from quaint shops and stores to farmland the farther I walk. But the walk itself is exhausting. And boring.

I'm about one step away from lighting up, even if it means risking getting busted, when I receive a message. I dig out my phone and read it, half-expecting it to be from that unknown number. But it's from Harlow.

Harlow: Hey! So, I forgot to tell you that if you ever need a ride to school or anything, just let me know. I usually drive myself, but sometimes my dad makes me use the driver. Either way, though, I'm cool with giving you a ride.

A driver? Holy freakin' what the crap?
Still ...

Me: Actually, I'd love a ride. That way I don't have to rely on my aunt or my cousin or take the bus.

Harlow: Yeah, you definitely don't want to take the bus. I've heard horror stories about them.

Me: I've rode the bus before, and I can

assure you that all those stories are probably true.

Harlow: I'll have to take your word for it, because there's no way in hell I'm ever going to ride the bus.

Me: Smart thinking.

Harlow: That's because I'm smart.

I'm smiling at this point, and it feels pretty damn good, even if the air is getting a bit chilly and my feet are starting to hurt.

Harlow: Also, I was wondering if you wanted to go to this thing with me this weekend. It's kind of like a club, but not really.

Me: Sounds a bit sketchy. ;)

Harlow: Not sketchy. Just mysterious.

While her texts are a little strange, it's not like I have anything better to do this weekend. Plus, it might be fun to get out and do something. And get away from The House of Horrors.

Me: All right, count me in.

Harlow: Sweet! And if you really want, you can invite my brother to go.

Me: Why would I do that?

Harlow: Oh, don't play stupid. I know you guys clicked at lunch.

She tops off the text with a smoochy face.

Me: We did not! We're just friends.

Harlow: Hmm ... You know there's an art to that sort of stuff, right?

Me: What sort of stuff?

Harlow: Just being friends with someone you're attracted to. And my brother, while an artist in many things, does not possess those skills.

I shake my head. She's getting confused. There's no way Hunter is attracted to me. And he was the one who said we should be friends.

Me: I really think you're getting this wrong. Your brother doesn't see me like that.

Harlow: Believe what you want, but it's totally true. And if you don't want to invite him, you don't have to. I just thought I'd throw the idea out there like a good BFF.

Me: Well, thanks, I guess.

Harlow: You're totally welcome. I gotta go. My dad is making me organize his files. TTYL

By the time we finish texting, I have a huge smile on my face. But that smile fades when I glance up and see that I've arrived at my house. Not that I'm not relieved that I no longer have to walk, but I have this unsettling feeling. Maybe because all the lights are off in the house. Or maybe because Dixie May hasn't gotten her revenge on me for not meeting her at lunch. Or perhaps it's because my aunt is pissed off at me.

Yeah, there's a lot of reasons for me to be skittish right now.

Sucking in a breath, I hike toward the front door, open it, and then enter. The instant I step over the threshold, my guard goes up. Only the hallway light upstairs is on. The air is quiet, too.

Where is everyone? Did they go out for a family dinner or something?

Pressing my lips together, I step inside, shut the door, and tiptoe for the stairway. I'm not even sure why I'm tiptoeing other than I don't want anyone to know I'm home. That is, if anyone is home.

Right as I reach the top of the stairway, I pause as my phone buzzes. I assume it's Harlow again, but nope. It's a text from Dixie May.

I almost don't read it, but curiosity gets the best of me.

Bitchy Bitch of the West: Found your little stash. Didn't know you were such a drug addict. Good thing my dad's a cop. Have fun in jail, beotch.

"No, no, no, no, no," I whisper in horror.

My heart slams against my chest as I rush to my room and shove the door open. The lamp is on, revealing the stash of drugs that I stole from my uncle scattered across my bed.

Shit.

I spin around to run, but my uncle steps out from behind the door and blocks my path, anger blazing in his eyes.

"So, you thought you could steal from me, huh?" He crosses his arms and stares me down.

He's not a very tall man, which is strange since my dad was really tall, but he's bulky and has a mean right hook. That I know personally. He's also still dressed in his sheriff uniform, even though he's probably been off work for a couple of hours. He wears it when he's trying to intimidate me. I don't know why he thinks it does.

"I didn't steal that from you." My voice comes out even. I've learned not to show fear when he gets like this. That it only seems to rile him up more. "That's stuff I bought." Yeah, I'm basically admitting that I bought drugs, but I'd rather have him believe that than know I stole from him.

He gives a hollow laugh as he steps toward me while reaching back for the door. "How stupid do you think I am, Raven? I'm well aware that you've been stealing from me. But do you want to know what pisses me off even more?"

I bite down on my tongue until I taste blood, resisting the urge to throw out some snarky remark.

He slowly closes the door, then *click*, he locks it. "That you know a little secret of mine."

I push down the fear wanting to emerge from inside me, let out a slow breath, and inch back. "I don't know anything."

"Liar." He matches my move, stepping forward and stealing the distance I put between us. "You've always been good at that—being a lying cunt." He steps toward me again, his fingers drifting toward his holster. "Remind me; have I marked you with that word yet? Sometimes it's hard to remember with all the marks I've put on you already." He pulls out his knife and flips the blade open. "You make it so easy with that mouth of yours. It's like you like me cutting you up."

Breathe in. Breathe out. Breathe in ...
Exhale.

"Look, I'm sorry for stealing your drugs. I don't know why I did it, but I'll stop. And I won't tell anyone about the stash you have. I'm a lot of things, but you know I'm not a narc."

He lightly traces his finger along the edge of the blade. "You know the only way I can get you to listen is to punish you. It's the only way you'll obey me."

He always says this, but it never makes any sense, since I rarely obey anyway. In reality, I wonder if he gets off on this, on seeing me in pain, which is so messed up.

"I'll start behaving better," I lie, the backs of my legs bumping against the bed as I take another step back.

Shit. I'm cornered, but I refuse to allow myself to panic.

Numb, Raven. Tune out that fear.

He shakes his head. "Don't lie to me again."

"I'm not lying, " I insist. "I promise. Just please don't cut me again."

His eyes flicker with delight for who the hell knows why. Then he reaches out and grabs my wrist. "You know I can do this. You know we have rules in my house."

"Why am I the only one who has to follow them?" I growl out, jerking on my arm. "Let go of me, you asshole."

A sinister grin curls at his lips. "And there she is." He shoves me down on the bed. "I don't know why you always try to pretend like you're obedient in the beginning. It never lasts. And you want to know why?"

I move to climb off the bed, but he wrestles me down, climbing on top of me and pinning me down. "Get off me!" I scream. "Now—"

He smacks me so hard my ears ring. Then he pins my hands down beside my head, leaning in and breathing into my face, "Because you're just like your stupid mother. You're a spoiled little brat who thinks you can do whatever she wants."

"Shut up!" I scream, tears pooling in my eyes.

"Aw, am I hurting your feelings? Well, good." Pinning both my hands in one of his, he leans back and lifts the hem of my shirt. "The next time you even think about trying to steal from me, you look down at this and remember." He points the tip of the blade at my side and nicks my skin, causing blood to pool out. "Remember what you are."

Then he starts cutting, moving the blade over my flesh. I barely feel the pain, though. I've become numb to this. Numb to everything.

Memories of my past—of the day my parents were murdered—begin to surface. It sometimes happens when I shut down like this. Although, it's always fragments of images that don't complete a full story.

Warm blood covers my hands as I stare down at my parents. Blood is all over them, covering their clothes, their hair.

Why is there so much blood? And why is it all over my hands?

"Mom," I whisper as I collapse to my knees.

I can't remember how I got here. Can't remember where the blood came from. All I can remember is screaming. So much screaming.

"Raven! No!" my mom shouts a plea. "Please don't do this, sweetie. You don't want to do this. Just go. Run!"

But I can't go. Not until I get to her.

"I'm sorry," I whisper. "I'm sorry I can't forget."

She screams—

"You're quiet tonight," my uncle says, yanking me back to reality.

Droplets of blood are on the blade of his knife and his hands.

Blood. Just like in my memories.

I never told anyone that I see myself covered in blood sometimes. If I did, I'd be under more suspicion. Maybe one day I can finally talk about it when all the dots are connected. I just hope I don't end up seeing something I don't want to.

Not wanting to think about my parents anymore, I focus on the pain in my side because it's easier than dealing with the emotional pain piercing inside me.

"Got nothing to say?" My uncle stands by my bed, staring down at me with expectancy.

I stare at the ceiling, not moving, refusing to say a word, refusing to give him the satisfaction of a fight, something I've learned he wants.

"Looks like it worked then." He wipes the blade of his knife across the side of his pant leg, cleaning off the blood. Then he puts the knife away and looks at me again, waiting for something. When I make no effort to even budge, he shakes his head. "Whatever. At least I got you to shut up." He moves to leave when his gaze zeroes in on my wrist. The wrist where the pendant he tried to burn is. His eyes flare with anger. "Where the hell did you get that?"

I swallow hard. "I found it in the yard at our old house."

Gritting his teeth, he yanks the bracelet from my wrist. "You fucking little thief. You're lucky I don't arrest you." With that, he storms for the door. "Don't ever touch any of my shit again," he snaps then walks out of my room, slamming the door behind him.

I don't move. Barely breathe.

I don't want to be here.

I want to fade away.

After what feels like hours, I drag myself off the bed and walk over to the mirror to see the damage. My side feels like it's on fire as I lift the hem of my blood-stained shirt and peer at the newly marked word branding my flesh. Then I shake my head, my jaw ticking.

He didn't only carve one word into my flesh, but three.

Disappointment.

Invisible.

Forgotten.

I lower my shirt, go to the bathroom, and clean and bandage the wound. Then I return to my room and sink down onto my bed, sitting in the middle of my drug stash that he just left in here, probably trying to send me some sort of cryptic message—my uncle really likes his mind games. What the message is, I haven't got a clue. And I really don't care.

Shoving the drugs out of the way, I lie down and close my eyes, trying not to think of anything other than sleep. Because sleep means forgetting. Of course, being an insomniac complicates that. So, eventually, and even though it's a bold move, I grab a joint and head over to my window.

I'm about to open it and light up when I spot someone creeping around in the backyard. As far as I know, my aunt and Dixie May aren't here, probably because my uncle sent them away so he could torment me in private. Dixie May thought telling her dad about my stash would lead to me getting arrested, so she's going to be severely disappointed when she realizes she's wrong.

I'm not sure if I am. If jail sounds any worse than what just happened.

I bounce back and forth between which one sounds worse as I watch the figure as it moves through the yard. At first, I think it's my uncle, going out there to try to burn the pendant again. But this person is moving like a stealthy ninja, and that's something my uncle definitely isn't.

If I cared, I'd tell my uncle, but honestly, part me hopes it's a car thief about to steal my uncle's car. But that hope gets squashed as the moonlight casts across the person at just the right angle so that I can make out their face ...

My jaw drops. "Hunter?"

What in the actual hell?

I watch as he moves closer to the house. He's wearing

all black, so it's hard to keep track of him, but his blond hair stands out against the darkness just enough.

After spying on him for a while and trying to figure out what the heck he's doing, I decide I'm just going to go out there. It could be a risky move, depending on if he's trying to rob us or not, but at this point, I don't really care.

Slipping on my jacket, I carefully step out of my bedroom and shut the door behind me. Then I tiptoe down the stairs, moving slowly, partly to be quiet and partly because my side hurts like a little beotch. When I reach the bottom, I sneak a glance toward the kitchen. The light is on, and I can see my uncle sitting at the table, staring at the pendant he jerked off me.

What's his deal with that thing? I hadn't thought about it too much when I picked it up, but with the way he acted when he saw it on me ... Something's up, and I want to find out what.

I make a mental note to look into it, even though I'm unsure where to start, then I quietly walk over to the front door and sneak outside. The front porch light isn't on, so I easily make my way around to the back without being seen.

Instead of stepping out into the open, I pause at the edge of the house and peer around for Hunter. He's gotten closer to the house, right beside it, and is hunkering down below the kitchen window where my uncle is.

At this point, I'm unsure how to proceed. I mean, the entire situation is bizarre.

"I'm not sure," Hunter suddenly whispers, startling me. "I can look through the window, but I'm worried someone is in there."

I squint against the darkness to see who he's talking to and manage to make out that he has what looks like his phone in his hand.

"I know," he whispers. "But ... I just don't want to get caught, okay?" He pauses again. "The only way to see if he's in there is to look through the window, but what if he's right there?"

Don't ask me why I do what I do next. Maybe my mind is so drained that I'm not thinking clearly. Whatever the reason, I say, "If you're talking about my uncle, he's right in the kitchen. And if you look through that window, he'll for sure see you."

Hunter lets out a string of curses then pauses. "Raven?"

"Yeah." I step out from my hiding space, and he moves out from underneath the window, straightening.

"What're you doing out here?" he asks, sounding on edge.

I inch toward him. "Shouldn't I be asking that question?"

"Yeah, you're right." He scratches the back of his neck. "Look, this isn't what it looks like."

"So, you're not trying to spy on my uncle?"

"Okay, maybe it is exactly what it looks like."

Crickets chirp in the distance as a beat of silence ticks by.

"So, are you gonna tell me why you're spying on my uncle?" I ask, breaking the silence.

"It's ... It's complicated," he says through a sigh.

"Well, I'm good with complicated stuff," I assure him.

"I'm sure you are," he mutters then releases a loud exhale. "Look, I can't give you all the details. All I can tell you is that I'm here because someone hired me to look into your uncle."

"Who?"

"I can't tell you."

"Okay ... Well, can you tell me why you're looking into my uncle?"

"Because he's the sheriff, and this person wants to know if he's corrupt."

I let out a low laugh. "I could've just told you that he is."

"Really?" he questions, but he doesn't sound that surprised.

"Yeah, really." I consider what I'm about to say, but not for very long. "What else do you want to know about him?"

"Everything, basically. It's difficult to find information

on him ... Honestly, it's almost like he's had a name change or something."

"If he has, I don't know about it." An idea is coming to me. One that I might not have acted on earlier before he carved *disappointment* into me. But now, well, I might as well live up to my name. "You want some help? I can try to look through his stuff for you instead of you trying to break in."

"I ..." He pauses. While I can't see his face, I'm sure he looks confused. "You'd do that for me?"

Would I?

Honestly, I'm not sure if I'm doing it for him or myself.

"I hate my uncle," I admit. "So yeah, I'll do it."

"You don't have to."

"I know. But I want to." I'm not even positive why I agree to this. Revenge maybe? Or to finally find out for myself who the man is that has taunted me since the day I moved in with him?

"How about this?" he says. "You sleep on it and let me know tomorrow."

"Okay," I agree with a nod.

"Okay." He grows silent again. "About seeing me out here ..."

I hold up my hand. "I'm not going to tell anyone."

"Thanks," he breathes in relief. "I owe you big time."

"Well, considering you bought me lunch and offered

to help me with art, we can probably call it even." When he doesn't reply, I quickly add, "Unless you don't want to do that yet."

He swiftly shakes his head. "No, I definitely do. I'm just ... You're being very nonchalant about this."

Am I? I guess I kind of am. "You just caught me at a weird time."

He's about to say something else when I hear a voice murmuring from somewhere. He curses and puts the phone to his ear, making me aware that whoever was on the call with him probably just overheard this entire conversation.

"What?" Hunter hisses. "Oh ... Why?"

While I can't see his face, I can almost feel his eyes on me.

"Let me ask her." He pauses, then snaps, "Dude, I'm not gonna do that. I'll *ask* ... Hey, Raven?"

"Um ... yeah?" I reply with a drop of apprehension.

"This is going to sound a bit weird, but I promise it's not," he starts. "I just ... Well, Zay, Jax, and I want to talk to you to really quickly."

"Like right now?"

"Yeah ... They're in my car, parked out in the forest right over there." He nods in the direction of the trees covering the landscape of the property bordering the yard.

I nervously fidget with the leather band on my wrist.

He wants me to go into the dark forest with him to meet up with his two friends, one who for sure hates me?

He steps toward me, and suddenly, I feel his hand cover mine. "I promise you'll be safe with me." He gently squeezes my hand.

I could quite possibly be a dumbass for trusting him, but the reality is that going into the house with my uncle probably isn't any less dangerous than going with Hunter. So, I nod.

"All right, yeah, I'll go."

"Awesome." He releases my hand. "Did I mention you're the best BFF ever?"

I giggle at that. "You know Harlow already claimed me as her best friend."

"We'll see about that," he teases, then takes my hand again and tows me with him as he hurries across the back-yard. "And FYI, you have the cutest giggle ever."

"I do not," I protest. "I don't even giggle."

"You totally do," he assures me. "In fact, you just did it one minute ago."

I scrunch up my nose. "Did I?"

"Yep. Don't worry; it's cute, not obnoxious."

Unsure what to make of what he says, I press my lips together, warmth rushing to my cheeks.

I'm blushing. I never blush. What the crap is wrong with me?

"Why do I get the feeling you're blushing right now?" he asks amusedly, his boots scuffing against the ground.

"I'm not," I lie, jogging to keep up with him, my side groaning in protest. But I ignore the pain, something I'm becoming a pro at.

"And now I get the feeling you're lying," he teases as he steers me into the trees.

I swat a few branches out of the way. "I never lie."

He snorts a laugh. "I call total bullshit on that."

I laugh, too. "Okay, it's total bullshit."

"Well, at least you're honest about that."

"Yeah, at least there's that."

We're both laughing at ourselves as the trees suddenly part and open up into a flat clearing. Without tree branches canopying above us, the moonlight cascades across the area. And parked right smack dab in the middle of it is Hunter's car. The lights are off inside, but I can make out the silhouettes of two figures, one sitting in the driver's seat and one sitting in the back. Jax and Zay, I'm guessing.

Hunter pulls me over to the passenger side and opens the door. Then he lets go of my hand. "You wanna sit in the back or the front?"

My gaze dances across the inside of the car. Now that I'm close, I see that Zay is in the driver's seat and Jax is in the back. Out of the two options ..."I'll sit in the back," I say then move to climb in, but he gently snags me by the elbow.

He leans in and whispers, "Zay's not going to be a dick to you anymore. I talked to him."

"Thanks," I tell him quietly, "but I still want to sit in the back."

"You think Jax is less scary, huh?" A bit of humor glitters his tone.

"Um ... He seems like it." I look at Hunter. "Is he not?"

Hunter wavers his head from side to side. "Most think he's not, but personally, I think his intense, quiet looks can be super frightening." He shudders.

I softly laugh under my breath.

"Dude, I heard that," Jax mumbles.

"That's good," Hunter throws back at him. "I'm glad to hear you're hearing is up to date."

Zay lets out the most frustrated sigh ever while Jax remains quiet.

Laughing at himself, Hunter motions for me to get in.

Sucking in a breath, I lower my head and climb into the back seat with him. He's sitting close to where I climbed in, leaving very little room on the seat.

"Shit. Sorry," he mutters then scoots over to the other side.

"You're fine," I tell him then plop down into the seat.

Hunter moves the seat back then slides into the passenger seat before shutting the door.

The scent of cologne and cigarettes touches my nostrils.

I wonder which one of them smokes?

"You got enough room back there?" Hunter asks, twisting around in the seat to look at me.

I nod, even though my legs are a bit cramped up. "I'm good."

"You sure?" he asks. "You have some really long legs."

"They're not that long," I insist, but he only chuckles.

"They're longer than average," he assures me. "But that's not a bad thing."

I still don't know if he's teasing me or not, but I attempt to pretend I don't have freakishly long legs, even though I know I do—I've been teased about them before. "Well, long legs or not, I have plenty of room," I lie.

"She's bullshitting you," Jax chimes in. "Her legs are pressed against the back of your seat."

"Oh." Hunter slides his seat forward.

My gaze snaps to Jax. "You little traitor." As soon as the words leave my lip, I want to retract them.

While I've spent today joking around with Harlow and Hunter, I don't know Jax at all. From what I could tell during class, he didn't seem like the type of guy who likes to joke around. But then the corners of his lips quirk upward.

"I may be a traitor, but at least your long-ass legs aren't folded up anymore."

"True." I stretch out my legs. "Though Hunter's probably are."

"Nah, he's got stubby legs," Jax quips, almost smiling again.

"What the hell is going on?" Zay abruptly says, rotating in his seat, his gaze skating between Jax and I.

Hunter is watching us with mild amusement as he answers Zay. "Well, I think our little Jax is finally having a bonding moment with someone."

Jax scowls at him. "Stop."

"What?" Hunter asks innocently.

Zay sighs and grumbles, "Jesus, here we go. We always have to have a comedy show going."

A giggle tickles at the back of my throat. I try to hold it back but fail epically. "You guys are funny."

Zay's hard eyes narrow in on me. "Don't encourage him."

"No, please do encourage me." Hunter grins at me, and I smile back. Then he smirks at Zay. "See? Raven thinks I'm funny."

"I'm pretty sure she doesn't," Zay disagrees. "I think she's just tolerating you."

They start arguing back and forth.

I glance at Jax. "Is this normal?"

Jax crosses his arms and shrugs. "Sort of."

"Oh." My brows dip together as I redirect my attention back to Hunter and Zay, who are now arguing about who ate the last of the cereal this morning. I have no clue how the subject shifted, but what I'm really starting to wonder is ... "Is this why you guys brought me here? To show me that you like to argue? Because, if so, point totally proven."

Jax chokes on a laugh then smashes his lips together.

Zay again narrows his gaze on me while Hunter just smiles and shakes his head.

"I think we're gonna have our hands full," he remarks, but I'm uncertain who he's speaking to.

Zay assesses me intently and with a hint of curiosity. "That we might be able to agree on."

"She should get bonus points for that, then," Jax suggests, uncrossing his arms.

"And maybe she should get bonus points for making you smile," Hunter retorts. "Twice."

I feel completely out of the loop, like they're talking around me. "I hate to break up this conversation and everything, but I really would kind of like to know why Hunter brought me here." I pause. "Not that I don't like learning all about you guys' little quirks, but we are sitting in the middle of the woods in the dark, so ..."

"Are you scared of the dark?" Zay questions, watching me.

I shake my head. "No, not really. It's more that I'm in

a car with three guys I barely know, one of which I know isn't a huge fan of me."

"You sat in my seat," Zay says like it explains everything.

"I didn't know it was your seat when I did it," I reply. "And the teacher told me they weren't assigned."

"Well, you could've moved when I asked you to," Zay points out, resting his elbow on the back of the seat.

"Maybe I could've, but in my defense, you didn't really ask. You just told me to move," I remind him. When his eyes narrow, I sigh. "Look, I'm sorry for being a pain in the ass, but I was just ... I don't know, a little nervous about it being my first day of school."

"You have a strange way of showing you're nervous," he says, his gaze dissecting me.

"I know," I agree. "I'm kind of a weird girl."

"Hmm ... I guess you should fit in well with us then," he mutters then blows out an exhale. "I'm sorry for snapping at you in class."

"Apology accepted." I stick out my hand for a fist bump.

He briefly stares down at my hand then looks up at me. "Yeah, you're definitely fucking weird." He fist bumps me then lowers his hand. "Now, on to the important stuff." He looks at Hunter. "How much did you tell her?"

"Not much," Hunter replies, slipping off his hoodie. "I told her why I was there—that someone hired me to look into her uncle and find out why his past is such a mystery."

Zay's gaze shifts back to me. "How did you even know Hunter was out there?"

I shrug. "I was standing in front of my window and saw him."

"Why were you standing in front of your window?" he questions, shoving up the sleeves of his shirt.

I give a half-shrug. "Because I was about to open the window and take a few hits."

He rests his arms on the back of the seat. "So, you're a pothead?"

"No. I don't get high all the time," I say, scratching my wrist. "Just when I'm stressed."

"And you were stressed out tonight?" he continues his interrogation on me.

I nod. "I got into trouble earlier and ... Well, yeah, I was freaked out."

"What sort of trouble?" Hunter asks, turning all the way around in his seat so he can look at me.

I hesitate, unsure how much I want to divulge about my life.

"If you want us to tell you our secrets, you gotta tell us yours," Zay informs me.

I glance from Hunter to him then sneak a glance at Jax, who's watching me, waiting for me to explain.

Is it worth it? My secrets in exchange for theirs?

Honestly, I really do want to find out more about why they're spying on my uncle. And it's not like I have to tell them everything, like about how my uncle cuts me.

"I may or may not have been stealing drugs from my uncle's secret stash," I offer the partial truth, then shrug like it's no big deal at all.

Hunter's lips part in surprise. "Okay, that's so not what I was expecting you to say."

Jax appears to be a bit shocked, as well. Zay doesn't seem to share the feeling.

"I'm not that surprised," Zay says, his gaze never wavering from mine. "So he found out you were stealing drugs from him and got pissed?"

I nod, tucking a strand of hair behind my ear. "It wasn't coincidental that he found out. Dixie May, my cousin, was pissed off because I didn't meet up with her at lunchtime to give her her makeup case."

"Dixie May?" Zay mutters confusedly. "Why does that name sound so familiar?"

"She's that ditzy blonde girl who tried to hit on you while we were taking a bathroom break during suspension," Jax tells him, brushing strands of hair out of his face.

"Shit. For reals?" Zay asks, looking at me.

I lift a shoulder. "Probably. I mean, I didn't see it happen, but you guys are all FH, so I'm sure she's probably going to hit on all of you." I bite down on my tongue, realizing I already told Hunter what that meant.

Zay's brows knit. "What's an FH?"

"Yeah, what does that mean?" Hunter asks me with a teasing grin.

Zay looks at me expectantly while Hunter just grins, totally amused with the situation because he knows exactly what it means.

Jax, however, is not looking at me expectantly. He's looking at me like he knows exactly what it means.

My cheeks warm, but since it's dark, they probably can't see, so I play it cool. "Now, what would be the fun in telling you?"

"Because then I'd know," Zay says, then looks at Hunter. "Tell me, man."

Hunter shoots me a playful look to which I respond with a teasing glare.

He smiles. So do I. I can't help it. His personality makes it impossible not to smile.

Zay looks between us with a crease between his brows. "Okay, would someone please tell me what the damn thing means."

A beat of silence ticks by where no one says anything, and then Zay huffs out a frustrated exhale.

"But anyway," I steer the conversation back to what we were talking about before. "Dixie May got pissed at me for the whole makeup case thing and told my uncle about how I stole from his stash. Though I have no freakin' clue how she knew I was stealing from him or where I hid all the drugs I stole."

"Could she have been spying on you?" Jax suggests.

"Maybe. She can be sneaky when she wants to," I say. "But I thought I was being sneaky, too. Plus, I hide everything I steal underneath a floorboard in my room. Well, I did before we moved … Maybe she saw me move it around when we moved."

"We can look into that later," Zay states, making me wonder how. Before I can ask, he continues, "What I want to know now is how your uncle didn't get busted. Because I'm assuming his drug stash came from him stealing a little bit here and there from the raids he did."

"How did you know that?" I wonder.

The edges of Zay's lips tug upward into a cocky grin. "Because I know a lot of things."

I arch my brows. "About cops?"

Instead of answering, he glances at Hunter and Jax. None of them say anything, and the silence makes me a bit squirmy.

Why does it feel like they're having a private conversation right now?

"How much do you know about Honeyton?" Zay asks, looking back at me.

"That it's a small town that's severely lacking in public transportation," I answer. "Seriously, I missed the bus today and had to walk home. In my old town, I could've just taken the city bus or called a cab. Well, if I had enough money."

"You walked home from school?" Hunter asks, sounding astounded.

I nod. "Normally, I ride with Dixie May, but her car is still getting transported here. So my aunt drove us to school this morning and was supposed to pick us up, but I sassed off to her this morning, so no ride for me."

Hunter frowns. "You should've texted me."

"You were at tryouts," I remind him. Not that I would've felt comfortable doing so.

"Yeah, well ... you could've called Harlow. Although she can be a little bit flaky when it comes to responding to her text." He gives a short, contemplating pause. "Zay and Jax are going to trade numbers with you, and if that ever happens again, you can text them." He pauses. "I think maybe you should just start riding to school with us."

Zay's gaze skates to him. "You really wanna bring her into this?"

"Into what?" I ask. "Because, while I've told you guys some things, you haven't really told me much."

Zay's attention returns to me. "Because we're not sure yet if we can trust you."

"You don't think I'm trustworthy?"

Am I trustworthy? I really don't know that part about myself, having not had any friends for a while.

"I don't know," Zay says. "You, your entire family, there's hardly any information available about you."

I frown. "You looked into my past?"

"No. But the person who hired us did a little bit and wants us to find out more," he explains, grazing his teeth along his bottom lip. "Well, not just you, but your whole family. Still ... it's strange that there's hardly any information online about you."

I swallow hard, wondering why there isn't. "What all did you find so far?"

They remain quiet for a thundering heartbeat of a second.

"Did you read about what happened to my parents?" I finally ask, my tone shaking a bit.

Again, they don't answer. But their silence is answer enough.

"I want to get out of the car," I say quietly. When they make no effort to move, I start to panic. "Let me the fuck out."

That snaps them out of their stare-down trance.

"Raven, calm down," Hunter says. "No one here is going to hurt you. And we don't have to talk about what happened to your parents. We just ... We just need to know why there's no information about you, your aunt, uncle, or even your cousin anywhere."

I'm not sure if I trust him or not, but truthfully, I'm

more caught up on what he said. "There's really hardly anything about us?"

He shakes his head. "I mean, there's a record of your uncle working for the police department at the last place he lived and a couple of addresses, but the information is extremely basic. And then you ..." He trails off.

"You're what we call a ghost," Zay finishes for him.

"I am?" I stupidly point to myself.

"The only things we could find were a few articles about your parents and a police record, but even that was sealed," Jax says, rotating toward me and bringing his leg up onto the seat. "It's very odd, but not completely unheard of in cases where people have gone into a witness protection program."

They settle into silence again, and it clicks.

I gape at him. "Wait ... you guys think I'm in the witness protection program?"

"We're not sure," Zay says. "But so far, it's all we've come up with."

"I ..." I shake my head. "No. There's no way."

"So you don't know if you are?" Jax questions, his gaze burrowing into me.

I shake my head again. "I ... I'm not. At least, not that I'm aware of. And I'm guessing if I was, I'd probably know, because I'd have to play a part."

They trade another look before their gazes settle on me.

"If you were, you'd lie to us," Zay tells me. "So, how do we know for sure if you're telling the truth?"

Panic trickles through me. "Well, I'm telling the truth. But even if I wasn't …" I sink my teeth into my bottom lip, going over all the self-defense moves I know. "What're you guys gonna do to me?" My shaky tone makes me cringe. I wanted to seem badass but messed that up.

Hunter looks taken aback. "What?"

"I think she thinks we're going to hurt her," Zay remarks, staring at me with intrigue.

"Well, we're not." Hunter sounds even more appalled. "Even if you were in the witness protection program, we wouldn't rat you out."

"But you said someone hired you to find out," I say softly, "so that means if you found out I—my family—was, wouldn't you have to tell them?"

When they don't answer right away, my pulse quickens.

"No, we wouldn't," Hunter says with certainty, eliciting a questioning look from Zay. Hunter glares at him. "We are not our fathers."

An uneven breath eases from Zay's lips. "Yeah, you're right." He scrubs his hand over his head. "This is all a moot point anyway, since we don't even know if they're in the witness protection program."

"I know, but I just want to make that clear," Hunter stresses.

They start talking back and forth about that while I try to decide if I'm in any real danger or not.

Jax must sense this, because he leans over and whispers, "You're fine. No one's going to hurt you."

I offer him a grateful smile, hoping he's telling the truth.

He gives me a small smile back then scoots forward in the seat and interrupts Hunter and Zay. "It's getting late," he tells them. "If we're going to convince her to help us, you two might want to start convincing her in a less frightening way."

Zay and Hunter look at him then back at each other.

"He's right," Hunter tells Zay. "If we want her to help us, we're gonna have to be upfront."

Zay drags his hand across his mouth, glancing at me and then at Hunter. "You want to tell her everything?"

"Well, not everything, since it'll take all damn night," Hunter says, "but we can tell her a little bit about what we do and let her sleep on that. Then, tomorrow, she can let us know if she wants to help us, and we can give her our whole background."

Their whole background?

I can't help thinking about how Katy made it seem like they were a mystery, and now they're saying they're going to tell me everything about them?

I wonder if it's true?

Zay deliberates for a moment before nodding. "Fine,

tell her. But only after we make a pact that what we say between the four of us, stays between the four of us. And if anyone breaks the pact, then they're out. Kicked out of the group. Finished—"

"Okay, we get the picture," Hunter cuts him off. "Jesus, Zay."

"I'm just trying to protect us," he stresses. "That's all."

Protect them from what, though?

"I know," Hunter says, his voice softening. "And making a pact is fine. You just don't need to be so intense about it." He looks at me. "Are you okay with making that pact?"

I nod without a drop of hesitation, since I have no one to tell and nothing to lose really. "Of course."

The edges of his lips tip up into a relieved smile then he looks at Jax. "Are good with that?"

Jax shrugs. "I have no problem with it."

Hunter bobs his head up and down then looks at me. "Honestly, you already know some of it already."

"You mean, like how you can track people's numbers and stuff?" I ask, scooting forward in the seat.

His lips quirk. "That's only a little bit of what we do. We can do a lot more things."

"What sorts of things?" I ask while folding my arms on the back of the seat.

"Oh, we can do a lot of things," Hunter says with a drop of playfulness in his tone.

Zay elbows him in the side. "Stick to the topic."

Hunter blasts him with a dirty look, but his expression softens when he returns his focus to me. "While we can track people's numbers—which FYI, we still need to work on yours more—our specialty is more PI type of stuff."

"PI ... As in a private investigator?" I ask with intrigue.

He nods, strands of his hair falling into his eyes. "Pretty much."

"Wow ... That's awesome, but weird," I say. "I mean, you guys are eighteen. How did you even get into this sort of stuff?"

"That's a question to ask tomorrow," Hunter explains. "For right now, all we need you to do is go back to your house and think about if you want to help us figure out why in the hell your family is off the grid."

"Unless you already know," Zay says, his gaze boring into me.

I carry his gaze. "I really don't. I didn't even know that until you guys told me." What I do want to know, though, is how much they were able to find out about me. They said they found a few articles about my parents, but do they know about my possible involvement in their deaths, or how I can't remember much about my past? While I'm not going to bring up the first, I can tell them the latter.

"I should probably tell you guys that I have some memory loss," I admit. "I can't really remember much about my past leading up to when I had to move in with my aunt and uncle."

"Really?" Zay asks, and I nod. "Why?"

I swallow the lump wedged in my throat then shrug. "I've never been officially diagnosed, but I did see a therapist once, and he suggested it was from the trauma of my ... my parents' deaths." I stare down at my lap, unable to look any of them in the eyes.

"Hey." Fingers brush across my chin, startling me.

When I glance up, I find that Hunter is the one who just touched me. He also has a soft smile on his face.

"You don't need to be ashamed of that," he says. "Trust me; all of us understand the whole having a traumatic past thing."

I swallow thickly. "Really?"

He nods, that kind smile remaining. "Yeah, really."

I'm unsure why, but for some reason that makes me feel better, as if I'm not as much of a freak as I thought. It's kind of a nice moment for me.

Well, until Zay mutters, "Shit."

He's looking at his phone.

Hunter flicks a glance at him. "What is it?"

He holds up the phone, showing video footage of what I think is the road that runs in front of our house. And on the road are headlights.

"You guys put a video camera up here?" I ask in surprise.

Zay lifts a shoulder like it's no big deal. "It's part of our protocol."

My lips form an O as I struggle to process everything.

"I know it's a lot to take," Jax says to me. "It'll get easier."

"If she agrees to help us," Zay intervenes. "If she doesn't, it might get complicated if she doesn't keep quiet about what she knows about us."

"I'm not gonna tell anyone, if that's what you're implying," I tell him, raising my chin in confidence. "I'm not a narc."

"Good to know you think so," he says with a smirk, "but I'll have to see for myself."

I narrow my eyes at him, about to smart off, when Hunter speaks first.

"I think that's your aunt's car," he announces. "We should probably get you back to the house."

"Good idea," I agree, because the last thing I need right now is to get busted for sneaking out. Though I'm not positive anyone would really care.

Still, they seem eager to leave, Hunter jumping out of the car and scooting the seat forward.

I duck my head to climb out, and then Hunter starts to shut the door.

"Wait," Jax says in a rush. "I thought we were going to trade numbers with her?"

Zay gives him a funny look. So does Hunter.

"I'll give her your guys' numbers while I walk her back to her house," Hunter tells him. "And I can give you hers."

"Okay." Jax relaxes in the seat.

Hunter closes the door, snags ahold of my hand, and guides me back into the trees. He remains silent for a while as we hurry back toward my backyard.

"You won Jax over pretty quickly," he abruptly remarks, moving a tree branch out of our way.

"I did?" I ask, nearly tripping on my face when I stumble on a rock. Luckily, Hunter has a hold of my hand and stops me from falling.

"He rarely talks to anyone, so yeah, I'd say you won him over pretty quickly."

"Is that a good thing or a bad thing?" I wonder as we reach the edge of my property.

He hunkers down low then moves forward, motioning for me to do the same. "It could be a good thing. Or a complicated thing."

"How?" I whisper as we near the back of the house.

He just shrugs, creeping over to the edge of the house and peering around the corner. "Looks like your aunt hasn't pulled up yet. You're good to go." He lets go of my hand and turns to me. "I'll send you everyone's number in a group text later tonight."

I nod. "All right."

He offers me a smile then moves to leave, but pauses

and twists back around. "Raven, if you ever need a ride or anything at all, even if it's just to talk, call us, okay? I know we haven't been friends for very long, but when we decide to let someone into our group, we decide that we're going to take care of them."

I nod, his words nearly overwhelming me.

I have friends. More than one. And they want to take care of me.

It's ... a lot to process, and I'll admit that I'm kind of wary about how long it'll last once they get to know me. Plus, what if I say I won't help them? Are they just going to ditch me?

I could ask him this, but all I say is, "How many people have you brought into your group?"

The moonlight highlights his smile. "You're the first." With that, he turns and slinks away into the night.

15

RAVEN

I MAKE it into the house before my aunt pulls up in the driveway. My uncle is still sitting in the kitchen when I enter and is staring at his phone while grumbling stuff underneath his breath. I quietly sneak up to my room and lock the door. About a minute later, I hear my aunt and Dixie May walk into the house, their loud voices carrying up the stairway. From what I can overhear, apparently, Dixie May was at cheerleading tryouts, and then the two of them went shopping.

Eventually, someone knocks on my door and I tense.

"Oh Raven, are you alive in there?" Dixie May asks from the other side. When I make no effort to respond, she says, "FYI, you can keep my makeup case. My mom bought me all new stuff today... You should try using some of my makeup. Maybe it'll help fix that hideous face of yours."

Again, I don't utter a word, lying on my bed and staring up at the ceiling. Eventually, she grows tired of taunting me and stomps off to her room.

One she's gone, I let out a breath and allow my mind to drift to Hunter and his friends.

What happened tonight seems so surreal, as if I dreamt it. Maybe I did. Perhaps this is all just a dream. If it is, though, I kind of want to stay in it since, for the first time in a long time, I don't feel so alone.

Still, I'm eager to know just who Hunter Hathingford really is, his background, why they're doing what they do? And Zay and Jax too. Are they spies? Detectives? Sure, Hunter tracked the number on my phone and said he learned how to from a PI, but he's also eighteen, and a spy or detective seems sort of out there—

I jolt as my phone buzzes.

Jesus, I'm jumpy tonight.

Telling myself to chill out, I pick up my phone, and then frown.

The message is from Unknown.

Unknown: I know something that you don't. It's about a little girl named Raven who lost something significant to her.

Attached to the message is a photo—a photo of the pendant my uncle just took from me.

I'd think it was my uncle who sent this message, but the pendant is lying in the snow, and we don't have snow here right now. However, there's a ton of snow in Wyoming, which makes me wonder if this photo was taken a long time ago. But then that leaves a lot of questions, starting with...

"Who the heck is this?" I mutter.

Unsure what else to do, I decide to text back and ask, even though I doubt they'll tell me.

Me: Who the heck is this?

Unknown: I'm your worst nightmare, little Raven. I'm the person who's going to make you pay for what you've done.

My brows knit at the mention of *little Raven.*

Why does that name sound so familiar...

Memories tug at my mind...

"Come here, little Raven," he whispers, the smell of blood touching my nostrils. "Let's see if you can fly—"

I blink, the memory shattering. My head pounds as I sink onto the bed, tears stinging my eyes.

I'm unsure what I saw or what it means, but what I do know is that at one point in my life, someone used to call me little Raven.

After massaging my temples for several minutes, the headache subsides, and I'm left wondering where the sudden onset of memories came from. And what does pendant has to do with anything? And more importantly, who the heck is messaging me?

I had thought moving here was a chance for me to start over and figure out my life. And while things are different, my life has gotten confusingly strange, as if me moving here set off something.

But what?

16

RAVEN

"You got that right swing down, right?" my dad asks as we cruise down the road in his old Camaro, music blasting from his iPod shuffle, his "old man music," as my mom calls it, playing from some speakers sitting on the back seat.

He's been working on fixing the car up but hasn't gotten very far yet. The leather seats are torn, the outside is primed but not painted, and the stereo is missing.

The windows are down, letting the warm summer breeze gust into the cab, blowing strands of my hair into my face as I nod and raise a fist in front of me. "Like this?" I swing against the air, hoping I've got the right form.

My dad smiles as he lifts his hand for a high-five, and I smile proudly as I tap my palm against his.

"That's the perfect form." He removes his cigarette from between his lips then ashes it out the window. "Keep *it up and you might just end up becoming a fighter when you grow up."*

"Like Momma?" I ask, crossing my fingers he'll say yes.

My momma is the coolest person I know. She's so tough. A lot of people think she's my sister, but my momma tells me that they only think that because she had me when she was young. I'm not even sure why anyone thinks she's related to me at all. She has blonde hair, where I have black; our eyes are different colors; and unlike hers, my cheeks are covered in freckles. I don't like my freckles that much. A lot of kids tease me about them. They say I look like I have dirt on my face.

"Yep, just like your momma." Dad puts his cigarette out in the ashtray then looks in the rearview mirror, messing with his scraggly brown hair.

My dad doesn't like to dress up. He wears a lot of old T-shirts and jeans. But today, he put on nice pants and a button-down shirt. He also made me wear a dress, which yuck, I hate dresses. The one I'm wearing right now is black. I'm glad for that because I hate bright colors, like pink, even more than I hate dresses. But I still don't get why he made me wear a dress or why my mom braided my hair. They usually let me do whatever I want. Today, though, they were all about me being on my best behavior while we go to wherever the heck we're going. My dad has also checked to make sure I remember how to swing a punch, like, a ton of times.

I don't know why he's asking this so much. I'm the only seven-year-old I know who knows how to throw a wicked right hook. I even got suspended from school once for hitting another kid. He deserved it for pantsing me. My parents thought so, too, and argued with the principal about it, which is why I no longer go to that school. Well, that and we moved recently.

The move had to do with me getting into the fight. At least, that's what I think I heard my parents whispering about late one night when they thought I was asleep. They were worried about me getting in too much trouble and drawing too much attention.

"All right, here we go," my dad mumbles as he pulls up to a set of tall gates.

We've been driving for what feels like hours and, until this gate, I haven't seen anything other than fields, trees, and old gas stations.

"Where are we?" I ask, kneeling up in the seat to try to see over the gates, but there are too many trees in my way.

Dad pushes the shifter into park and stares at the gates with a frown on his face. He's not usually the kind of guy who frowns a lot, so it's weird to see one on his face.

"Dad?" I say when he doesn't seem like he's going to answer me. "What is this place?"

He glances at me. "This, Ravenlee, is a stipulation."

"Am I in trouble?" I ask, glancing at the gate again. He only calls me Ravenlee when he's mad at me or stressed out.

He shakes his head. "No, you're not in trouble. If anything, I am."

"Why?"

He shrugs. "I don't know ... It's ..." He offers me a smile. "You don't need to worry about it. This is grown up stuff. All you need to worry about today is making sure that, if anything bad happens, you swing your fist like your life depends on it, got it?"

I nod, wanting to make him proud of me. "Got it."

He starts to smile, but it fades when the gates start to open.

Sighing, he drives forward through the entrance and turns onto a paved driveway that leads to the biggest house I've ever seen.

"Whoa, who lives here?" I ask with my nose pressed against the window.

The house is so huge that it has three floors.

"A business acquaintance," my dad replies as he pulls up to the front doors.

Two guys are standing on the front porch, and just behind them is a kid around my age with hair so blonde it nearly looks while. Even with how far away he is, I can tell he looks sad.

I turn to my dad. "Is that boy your business acquaintance?"

Shaking his head, he puts the shifter into park, turns off the engine, and then hesitantly reaches for the door. "No."

He's being really weird. It makes me worry, even though he said I don't need to. I want to ask him questions, but he opens the door and climbs out.

I'm not sure if I'm supposed to follow him or if I should stay in the car.

"Come on, Ravenlee," he says then closes the door.

He called me Ravenlee again.

Something's wrong.

But I get out anyway, trusting my dad, and hurry around to the front of the car where he's waiting for me. He takes my hand when I reach him then pulls me with him as he starts up the pathway toward the guys.

"You made it," the taller one says to my dad. Then his gaze flits to me. "And you brought the little raven."

My dad's hold on my hand tightens. "I didn't really have a choice, did I?"

The man stares at me for a beat with eyes a strange color of grey, like storm clouds, then he looks at my dad. "No, you didn't." Again, the man with stormy eyes glances at me.

He's starting to make me feel really squirmy, so I look at the boy instead.

He looks even sadder up close, so I smile at him. And

for a moment, he smiles back at me. But then his smile shifts to worry as the man with stormy grey eyes looks at him.

"Go and get the others," he tells him.

The kid nods then looks at me for a fleeting moment before hurrying inside the house.

The man looks back at my dad and opens his mouth to say something when lightning snaps across the sky and thunder immediately follows—

My eyelids pop open as I suck in a sharp breath. My skin is damp with sweat, my hair feels gross, and the wound on my side throbs as I stare up at my bedroom ceiling.

That dream I just had ... or was it that? The guy had called me little raven, just like the unknown sender did. Could it have been a... memory? One of my forgotten ones?

"No, it had to be a dream," I mutter, but doubt weighs on my mind.

I can't get rid of the inkling that it was a memory, and that the place I was at—that huge house—was located in Honeyton. I'm unsure why, though.

And what about the boy with hair so blond it looked white... Just like Hunter's did tonight in the moonlight?

Perhaps I'm just reaching. Yeah, I have to be. There's no way I once met Hunter. I'd remember that.

Then again, my mind is filled with a lot of holes.

Pressing my lips together, I open my phone and do something that makes me feel slightly guilty. I search online the name: *Hunter Hathingford.*

What I find is... well, I'm not sure because I can't find anything about him or about anything that has to do with his last name. Hunter does know how to trace phone numbers, though, so maybe he has the knowledge on how to wipe all traces of his records? It seems plausible, but why would he do that?

Why would he not want anyone to be able to find anything about him?

ALSO BY JESSICA SORENSEN

A Pact Between the Forgotten:

The Art of Being Friends

The Rules of Being Friends (coming soon)

Signed with a Kiss Series:

A Truthful Kiss

Whispered Secrets & a Kiss (coming soon)

The Undercover Files:

Discovering Benton

The Start of a Road Trip (coming soon)

The Honeyton Mysteries:

Chasing Hadley

Falling for Hadley

Holding onto Hadley

Untitled (coming soon)

Rebels & Misfits:

Rules of a Rebels & a Shy Girl

Untitled (coming soon)

Rebels & Misfits Detectives:

Spies, Lies, & Cupcakes

Untitled (coming soon)

My Cursed Superhero Life:

Cursed

Untitled (coming soon)

Capturing Magic:

Chasing Wishes

Chasing Magic

ChasingPromises

Untitled (coming soon)

Tangled Realms:

Forever Violet

Untitled (coming soon)

Curse of the Vampire Queen:

Tempting Raven

Enchanting Raven

Alluring Raven

Untitled (coming soon)

<u>**Unraveling You Series:**</u>

Unraveling You

Raveling You

Awakening You

Inspiring You

Every Single Breath

Untitled (coming soon)

<u>**Unexpected Series:**</u>

The Unexpected Complications of Revenge

Untitled (coming soon)

<u>**Shadow Cove Series:**</u>

What Lies in the Darkness

What Lies in the Dark

Untitled (coming soon)

<u>**Mystic Willow Bay Series:**</u>

The Secret Life of a Witch

Broken Magic

Stolen Kisses

One Wild, Crazy, Zombie Night

Magical Whispers & the Undead

Untitled (coming soon)

<u>**Standalones:**</u>

The Illusion of Annabella

The Forgotten Girl

<u>**The Heartbreaker Society:**</u>

The Opposite of Ordinary

Untitled (coming soon)

<u>**Broken City Series:**</u>

Nameless

Forsaken

Oblivion

Forbidden (coming soon)

<u>**Guardian Academy Series:**</u>

Entranced

Entangled

Enchanted

Entice

The Forest of Shadow and Bones

Untitled (coming soon)

<u>**Sunnyvale Series:**</u>

The Year I Became Isabella Anders

The Year of Falling in Love

The Year of Second Chances

Untitled (coming soon)

The Coincidence Series:

The Coincidence of Callie and Kayden

The Redemption of Callie and Kayden

The Destiny of Violet and Luke

The Probability of Violet and Luke

The Certainty of Violet and Luke

The Resolution of Callie and Kayden

Seth & Greyson

The Evermore of Callie & Kayden

Untitled (coming soon)

The Secret Series:

The Prelude of Ella and Micha

The Secret of Ella and Micha

The Forever of Ella and Micha

The Temptation of Lila and Ethan

The Ever After of Ella and Micha

Lila and Ethan: Forever and Always

Untitled (coming soon)

Ella and Micha: Infinitely and Always

<u>The Shattered Promises Series:</u>

Shattered Promises

Fractured Souls

Unbroken

Broken Visions

Scattered Ashes

<u>Breaking Nova Series:</u>

Breaking Nova

Saving Quinton

Delilah: The Making of Red

Nova and Quinton: No Regrets

Tristan: Finding Hope

Wreck Me

Ruin Me

<u>The Fallen Star Series:</u>

The Fallen Star

The Underworld

The Vision

The Promise

The Lost Soul

The Evanescence

The Mist of Stars (untitled)

The Darkness Falls Series:

Darkness Falls

Darkness Breaks

Darkness Fades

The Death Collectors Series (NA and YA):

Ember X and Ember

Cinder X and Cinder

Spark X and Spark

Unbeautiful Series:

Unbeautiful

Untamed